HERO LOST
MYSTERIES OF DEATH AND LIFE

An Insecure Writer's Support Group Anthology

FREEDOM FOX PRESS
Dancing Lemur Press, L.L.C.
Pikeville, North Carolina
www.dancinglemurpress.com

Copyright 2017 by The Insecure Writer's Support Group
Published by Freedom Fox Press
An imprint of:
Dancing Lemur Press, L.L.C., P.O. Box 383, Pikeville, North Carolina, 27863-0383
www.dancinglemurpress.com

ISBN: 9781939844361

All rights reserved. No part of this publication may be reproduced, transmitted, or stored in a retrieval system in any form – either mechanically, electronically, photocopy, recording, or other – except for short quotations in printed reviews, without the permission of the publisher.

This book is a work of fiction. Any resemblance to actual events or persons, living or dead, is coincidental.

Cover design by C.R.W.

Library of Congress Control Number: 2017931860

The Insecure Writer's Support Group would like to thank the judges who selected the stories for this anthology. We appreciate their time and effort!

Elizabeth S. Craig - Cozy mystery author for Penguin Random House, Midnight Ink, and independently.

Richard Harland - Author of seventeen speculative fiction novels.

Laura Maisano - Senior editor at Anaiah Press for their YA/NA Christian fiction

Russell Connor – Author and owner of Dark Filament Publishing Startup

Dawn Frederick – Literary agent and the founder of Red Sofa Literary

Ion Newcombe - Editor and publisher of AntipodeanSF, Australia's longest running online speculative fiction magazine.

Lynn Tincher - Author, public speaker, and executive producer.

Table of Contents

The Mysteries of Death and Life by Jen Chandler............7
The Silvering by Ellen Jacobson...................................27
Memoirs of a Forgotten Knight by Renee Cheung..........47
Sometimes They Come Back by Roland D. Yeomans.....62
The Wheat Witch by Erika Bebee................................81
The Last Dragon by Sarah Foster...............................102
Mind Body Soul by Elizabeth Seckman......................122
Captain Bulat by Olga Godim....................................142
The Witch Bottle by Sean McLachlan........................162
The Art of Remaining Bitter by Yvonne Ventresca.......175
Of Words and Swords by Tyrean Martinson................191
Breath Between Seconds by L. Nahay.......................207

The Mysteries of Death and Life
by Jen Chandler

Part I

Gaston was dying. I suppose I knew it when I first met him. The truth of it hit home the second time I climbed the old church steps. One crumbled beneath me and splintered stones to the rubble below. In the shafts of moonlight they looked like falling stars.

He'd been there months before I found him, moldering in a corner, festering sores over his mouth and eyes. Completely blind, he feared me at first until I convinced him I was only human. I wanted to help and I guess, in a way, I did. At least I like to think that I did. The only thing I'm certain of is that Death saved me.

"Stay away" he whispered, his lips cracked and bleeding. "I'll fail you."

I laughed, nervously, and he cocked his head, as if listening for a far-off bell.

"Do that again," he said. Try as I might, I couldn't without it sounding artificial.

"No matter," he settled back. "Those sounds stop eventually and all you're left with is pain."

It took two weeks before he'd touch water. I left little glasses for him at each visit and found them untouched when I returned. I was convinced he'd die of thirst, but that's not what took him. Not what was the matter. I think the only reason he finally drank was to pacify me and my constant worrying.

"You've got to drink," I told him. "You'll die if you don't."

"If only it was that easy." He choked on a laugh.

HERO LOST: MYSTERIES OF DEATH AND LIFE

He looked at me with unseeing eyes and groped for a glass. I took his hand and he flinched. His skin felt like old silk and I suppressed a shudder. With the glass between his long, frail fingers he sipped, wincing as the cold water touched his lips.

"I've brought balm," I offered, as he finished off the water and put the glass down with a clank. It teetered and fell, rolled a bit.

Without asking, I scooted closer, careful not to scrape my knees on the broken, colored glass scattered about. Dabbing my finger into the goop, I tried to gently apply a glob. Gaston jumped, fell backwards, hit the wall with a thud.

"Whoa, easy. It'll help."

"I don't want help." His voice thick, he turned from me, lost again to whatever inner world he inhabited.

"You need help." I stood and let the balm fall at my feet. "The balm is here. Find it for yourself if you care."

Life kept me away for six days. Convinced I'd return to a corpse, I ran off at sunset and ducked under the yellow tape and warning signs, squeezed through the chained gate, and slid through the boards blocking off the old doors.

"Hello?" My voice bounced around the vestibule.

The pigeons cooed and stirred in the rafters, mothed their ways through a hole in the roof. I jumped, startled, and climbed up the staircase to the attic. He was still there, lying on his back facing the shattered window, a lost work of art.

"At night," he said when I reached the top step, "when the clouds pack off, I can see the stars again." His eye lids glistened. The balm tin was at his feet. He'd used it after all.

"You said you were blind." I walked over, squatted beside him.

"Not here," he pointed at his face. "Here." His

THE MYSTERIES OF DEATH AND LIFE

hand went to his heart. "Feel." he took my hand and put it on his chest.

Nothing. There was nothing. Wrenching my hand I flicked backwards and he scoffed.

"Are you afraid of death?" he asked, propping up on an elbow.

"No." I shuffled my feet. "Yes. Yes, I suppose I am."

"And yet you visit me often."

"You're dead?"

"No. I'm Death."

Part II

For days I told myself he was crazy, just another homeless bum. But the nights brought daydreams of coal black wings, of far off songs that hinted at hope. I could better cope with my own situation, my own homelessness. I knew he was real, knew I wasn't dreaming. Knew neither of us was mad.

"How can you be Death and be dying?"

I sat across from him as he tried some of the cheese I'd brought. It was all I could smuggle out that morning. He nibbled the cheese, made a face.

"Gave up." He put the cheese back on the napkin. "The job got to me and I walked away."

I pushed the water glass towards him. "So you quit. 'Angel of Death resigns, news at 11.'"

He laughed, a raspy, rusty gate hinge that hurt just to hear. "Something like that."

"Who took your place?"

Sadness shook his head and he stuck his finger in the water glass. Round and round it went creating ripples until they sloshed about and rained down the edges like the tears that formed in the corners of his glassy eyes.

"No one. It's mine and I'm it." His laughter cut sharp and cynical. "I'm. It."

"What does that mean?"

"Mean?"

"For the dead? The dying? Who takes them now?"

"Nobody takes them. I don't take them. They come or they don't. It's their choice. The last choice any human ever has to make."

Somehow he perceived my frown. "What? You thought I appeared with a sickle? All black robed and skeletal?" His laugh turned to coughing and I moved to help him. He put up a thin, scabbed hand. "Another misconception," he wheezed.

We sat in silence. Somewhere a garbage can clanged and a dog whined. My skin prickled at the approaching storm. "And if someone decides they don't want to go?"

He continued moving his finger in the water. A breeze came through the broken window and leaves swirled about my knees. Downstairs something creaked. I jumped, turned, expecting to see someone on the stairs, but there was no one.

Gaston stopped pushing the water around. "You've heard of ghosts haven't you?"

He'd given me a lot to think about that night. A storm closed in and I had to get back to the shelter. I'd begged him to come with me, to get medical care from the clinic, but he refused. Hot meals and bandages weren't at the top of his agenda. What was? I asked him that before I left and he threw the glass of water at me, narrowly missing my face. I decided I wouldn't ask again.

Part III

Nightmares plagued my sleep and I woke around two. The dreams didn't make sense and were little more than images, haunting images of people lost and wailing. I sat in bed, in the dark, listening to

THE MYSTERIES OF DEATH AND LIFE

the breathing of the three other women I shared a room with. The shelter wasn't much to look at but it was dry, warm, and mostly peaceful. At least I didn't have to worry about anyone trying to attack me in an alleyway.

I slipped out from the covers, found my sneakers and the hoodie they gave me the first night I'd arrived. The linoleum gleamed under the red EXIT sign but no other light came in. The storm still grumbled. I wondered if Gaston was satisfied with himself, Death and dying in an abandoned church. The bizarre realization that I'd spent the last few weeks with the Angel of Death wrapped around my gut, filling me with the strange sense that something was going to be required of me. You didn't just acquaint yourself with a celestial being without some sacrifice. All the old stories told me that.

I sat at one of the dining hall tables and pulled out a crumpled piece of paper. Clean paper was a luxury I'd not had in years and I magpied as much as I could. Fishing in the other pocket I found the stub of pencil I'd clung to since Dad walked out and Mom died in a place a lot worse than this.

Gaston's Story I scrawled underneath a couple of crossed out lines. No. The eraser long gone, I scribbled through it again. *The Man in the Church.* Scratch. *Death Chooses the Die.* Scribble. No. None of it. Compelled to tell his story I ignored the title and began writing.

Sometime around five I heard the ladies in the kitchen arrive. The pans clanked and clattered as they readied themselves to feed breakfast to the fifty-two residents. I sifted through some old fliers shoved in one of the office trashcans and eked out several pages. They weren't fantastic but they were mine. Perhaps I'd show them to Gaston. Maybe I'd read them to him. Then again, maybe he'd be in a foul mood and ignore me. He had a nasty habit of doing that.

I'd lied to the director for weeks. One of the things the shelter prides itself on is pushing its residents to find work, to not live off the system. And I'd looked, honestly, for the first few months and found nothing. Nada. Well, OK, I did get hired at McDonald's, but after the fry cook tried to drag me behind the dumpster, I'd quit and not been able to find anything since. People write about people like me, about "statistics" and "sad cases," but they don't know the truth. They don't know your father worked his entire life only to be made redundant, lost his forced retirement in a "sure thing" investment, and died in an alcoholic ward. They don't know that your mother taught dance until your father's implosion lost them their independence.

Breakfast came and went quietly. The other girls went to work or to the employment agencies. My counselor asked if I had any new leads.

"One," I said. "Just one."

"Oh? And where is it? You know I can put a good word in for you."

I nodded, shrugged. "It's only a thought right now, Julie. I promise when it's something more I'll tell you."

"You can't spend your entire life cleaning the rooms here."

"I know." And I did. But there was something more driving me than just the hunger and thirst for independence. It was a fragile, skeletal dream that drove me back to Gaston's perch, high in the bell tower of the collapsing Methodist church. I pocketed some French toast sticks and one of those plastic things of watered down juice and set out to the overgrown church yard.

The tall, wet grass stuck to my jeans. Mud sucked at my shoes and I kicked them off in the entryway, making sure to tuck them safely behind one of the

THE MYSTERIES OF DEATH AND LIFE

loose boards that lined the wall. If anyone decided to poke around, I didn't want them finding my shoes. The last thing I needed was to try and explain that I was visiting the Angel of Death in an abandoned church. I'd end up on floor three of Memorial in a white jacket. I knew something had to shift, had to change, and I'd convinced myself that was up to Gaston.

The place smelled rancid, like pee and old cake. I shuddered. I'd brought the cake the week before. A rat scuttled past me as I entered the bell tower.

"Gaston?" I whispered. Strange how voices echo in churches, take on new dimensions.

I heard a rustle and knew it was him. I'd managed to filch some more antibiotic salve from the nurses' station and knelt in front of him to put some on. He jerked his hand back.

"You've got to let me do this for you."

"I don't want to get better."

"You're being childish."

He laughed, coughed and spat across the room. "I never had the luxury of being a child. I've gathered many, though. Many that should have grown old, many that should have had the same chances and the same..."

"Now you're being pitiful."

"Pitiful?" He lunged for me, grabbed both my arms and pulled me to him.

I cringed. His face was caked in blood that came from where his eyes should have been. "Pitiful? Yes, I am! I AM DEATH and I can't even kill myself!"

He let me go and I scrambled backwards. His long fingernails scratched my arms and I untied the hoodie around my waist and pulled it on. Julie would pounce at those if she saw them. I planned to leave and remembered the French toast and juice.

"Here. Not that you'll eat it. Not that you care if I got caught, I could be kicked out of the shelter." I shoved the napkin and the juice at him. "Not that you care about anyone but yourself!"

I turned to go, angry that I'd ever taken a chance on someone like him.

Someone like me.

I stopped at the top step. Odd to think an angel could be anything like me. But he was. A blight on humanity some call us. A sad state of affairs. But the truth is we're really just like the rest of you, the rest of them. We've just got further to climb and it's harder for us to decide to reach.

Gaston sniffed. He was crying. Was it even possible to cry without eyes?

I went back to him, knelt beside him, hesitantly put a hand on one shoulder. I jerked back automatically. There was a ridge at his shoulder blade, a bit of bone that protruded. It occurred to me that must be where his wings used to be. I ran my hand across his upper back and, yes, there was another one. Two bony ridges where the glory of heaven used to sit.

"What happened?" I whispered as he wailed. "What happened to make you walk away?"

He stretched out, lay his head in my lap, didn't bother to wipe his face. "I fell in love."

Part IV

Gaston told me of Monica, of how he'd seen her at her uncle's funeral. He was used to family members cursing his name, but she stood smiling at her uncle's coffin. When everyone else left Monica stayed. She stayed as the gravediggers shoved dirt over the wooden top. Stayed as the clouds began to cry. All night long she sat in the mud, watching over her uncle's grave. That's when he broke the Rules and spoke.

"She was afraid, then adjusted. She said she felt safe. With me. With Death. She told me how her uncle

THE MYSTERIES OF DEATH AND LIFE

and aunt raised her when her parents died. How they loved her like a daughter. I remembered her aunt; she was a fine lady. The uncle was polite, serenely nodded when I came for him. Monica had no one. She was alone. I told her I could help her. I could take her to her aunt and uncle." Gaston hung his head and sighed. "Oh how foolish I've been."

"You offered to kill her?"

"I offered her the Choice. To go or stay. Only in this case, it was an offer of death or life, not of wandering or rest."

"I don't understand."

He sat up, propped himself on one thin arm and faced me. "The dying can choose between rest or wandering. To offer the same choice to the living..."

It started to click. He lay back down and I said, "They can either die or live forever."

He nodded.

"What did she choose?"

Again he began to cry and I knew. I stroked Death's head and the sky thundered. I thought for a moment it might be God, calling Death home.

Part V

Early the next morning, I slipped from my room and padded into the dining hall. The night before, I'd asked Julie for more scrap paper and a phone book and she obliged. When she asked what I was doing, I told her I was writing a story. Surprisingly she didn't laugh. She smiled and said she'd like to read it when I finished. I only nodded and scooted away. I looked up every Monica I could find in the phone book. There were seventeen. I wrote down their addresses. She had to live local. Why else would Gaston choose his specific run down tomb? Eight of the addresses were outside the city limits so I decided to start with the others.

It was a mini bus tour of the nicer side of the city. Four of the remaining nine weren't home. Two refused to answer the door. One threatened to call the cops. Out of the last two I had to choose. It was almost dinner time and if I wasn't back soon they'd worry, and send the cops to search for me.

I closed my eyes and let Fate decide. The bus took me to the end of an old street with old houses and even older trees. It felt right. The rusted copper address hung next to the bell. It echoed through the house. A lovely woman of indeterminate age answered the door. She had long dark hair and dark, haunted eyes.

"Monica?" I asked. She only stared.

"My name is Leah. I'm a friend of Gaston."

She blinked, looked up and down the deserted street. Then her eyes closed and she let out a deep sigh.

"Please," she smiled softly. "Come in."

Her movements reminded me of my mother, all grace and poise. Monica brewed lavender tea and her house smelled like Spring. There were flowers everywhere. She guided me to a sun room, all shimmering glass and bromeliads. I struggled against tears. Lavender was my mother's favorite. When I told Monica, she reached out and put a hand on my arm.

"Your mother's gone?"

I wiped my face with the back of my hand.

"Mine too. Everyone I've ever loved is gone. Except Gaston."

"He's dying." I looked her in the eyes.

She didn't blink. "He told me that's what he wanted."

"Only he can't. It must be a rule or something."

We made quite a study in opposites: Monica dressed in white, her hair stark against it; me, dressed

THE MYSTERIES OF DEATH AND LIFE

in dingy grays, my dirty blond hair morphing with the limp hood that sat against my shoulders.

"I wonder at your story, Leah. You said you were from the shelter?"

I shrugged one shoulder. "My parents are gone. My mother died in a horrible place. They shut it down because of negligence and I was carted off with the rest of them. I'm thankful though. They're kind there, try to help. I'm supposed to find work but..."

"It's hard on that side of town. Have you thought of looking here?"

"Here?" My eyes went wide. "No one would hire me here. We're given one set of nice clothes and even those aren't nearly nice enough to warrant an open door here."

"What about college?"

"Dunno. I mean, I could. They'd help me get into the technical school but, well..." I fingered the hem of my old blue button-up.

"But what?" Her eyes held interest and for a moment I forgot why I was there.

"I want to write, see. My mother told me her mother was a poet and her mother wrote novels. Penny-dreadful sort of things, but they were published for a while."

"And your father?"

I chewed the inside of my mouth. "He lost it all, then lost it."

She nodded. "I'd like to read your stories."

"Well, there's only one and it's not quite finished." I looked up from my cup. "It's about Gaston."

"Ah." Monica sipped her tea and I did likewise. It was warm and fragrant, nothing like the little teabags at the shelter. This was delight, music on my tongue. I rolled the liquid around and around, desperate not to forget.

"He's in a church?"

HERO LOST: MYSTERIES OF DEATH AND LIFE

I nodded. "The bell tower of the old Methodist church off Cornwall."

"It used to be so beautiful there. My aunt and uncle are buried in the cemetery. I haven't been there in...years."

"It's all weeds and thorns. I wish I could save it. That whole area could be so beautiful. Right on the borderlands. A dividing block between East and West."

"The stained glass sang on Sundays," Monica whispered. "You could hear the organ resonate off the panels if you pressed your ear close enough."

"You went there?"

She nodded. "My aunt and uncle were founders. If the brass plates are still there, look beneath the window with the dove."

"I will." I sipped again and braved on. "What about Gaston? Will you come see him?"

"I don't think so. It's my fault."

"He doesn't blame you. He blames himself."

She laughed a little. "He would."

"Just one visit. I'll meet you there. It's really dirty and kinda dangerous but the stairs are still strong. We could find your aunt and uncle's graves. I'll bring flowers. There's some fake ones in the dining hall. No one would notice if I took a few."

She smiled and stood. "Come with me. I want to show you something."

I reluctantly left my cup and followed her up a flight of stairs.

It was a library. The most beautiful sight I'd ever seen. Books lined every wall and there was a ladder like in the old movies. A sky light let in the diffused sun and spirits of dust parted as Monica moved to the center of the room. She watched me a moment and laughed.

"Impressed?"

THE MYSTERIES OF DEATH AND LIFE

All I could do was nod.

"I've had a long time to amass this collection. Many of the oldest belonged to my uncle but I've done my fair share of pond-hopping to find some others." She wandered to one of the shelves and let her long, elegant fingers trip along the spines. I was afraid to touch anything, afraid to contaminate the soft leather and gentle cloth, afraid they'd burst to nothing if I so much as breathed.

"Here we are." The book she brought over was dilapidated.

"It's a Bible," I said as she held it to me.

"Go on. It won't bite. And you can't hurt it. It's already falling apart."

I gently held it, cradling it, a great treasure to luxury deprived fingers.

"And it's not a Bible. Look."

I couldn't read the title. Monica suddenly realized this and laughed, more at herself than me. "I'm sorry. I don't get many visitors anymore. Sometimes I forget most people these days don't read outside their own language." She ran her fingers across the title. "*The Book of Celestial Beings*. It's French. Open it."

I pulled back the heavy cover, turning like breath so the moth wings wouldn't tear.

"There," she pointed and I gasped. She read, "'Compiled by Gaston d'Morte.'"

"He wrote a book?"

"He compiled the stories of angels. This is the only copy. I'm not even supposed to have it."

She read the question in my glance, smiled. "He left it with me the last time I saw him."

I ran my fingers across his name. "When was that?"

"Five months ago. He came to ask me again what I choose. Again I didn't give him an answer."

I looked at her, frowning. "If you didn't choose,

HERO LOST: MYSTERIES OF DEATH AND LIFE

how are you still here?"

"His doing. The Choice shouldn't be offered to the living. I'm in limbo, you see. Not ready to die and not sure of living. I've amassed great fortune and a number of beautiful things and yet I haven't really done anything. He pointed this all out of course. And when he asked, I refused an answer."

"Then there's still time. You could save him." I looked at her, at the sadness in her eyes. "And yourself."

"I'm afraid." She whispered, looking at her nails. "I have no one. No family, no children. All of this is a waste."

"No, no it isn't! You can do a lot of good! Give it away, start a fund, find someone to leave it all to."

"Death is final."

"Yes." I nodded. "It is. But for now you're still alive. A choice, to live or exist, you can change that at any moment." I put the book on a table and began to thumb through it. I came to a page illuminated with gold dust and light. "Then again, maybe death isn't final. He wrote this book, didn't he? Touched these pages, your heart. Mine."

Monica came and stood beside me. "'The Mysteries of Death and Life.'" She read. "Gaston lettered that himself. He used to practice for me, used my paints and brushes." She pointed to a framed print over the fireplace. "That was the last one he did."

I wandered over to look. It was unsigned but dated 1802.

"How old are you?" I closed the book and looked at her.

"Not that old, really."

The grandfather clock chimed downstairs. "I have to go. If I'm not back by 5:30 they send out the hounds."

She smiled and walked me downstairs.

THE MYSTERIES OF DEATH AND LIFE

"Your house is very beautiful," I told her as we stood on the porch. "Think about what I said, please. You've got so many amazing books in there. I'm sure someone would be happy to keep them for you. Find someone deserving. And come see Gaston."

I ran to meet the bus that was pulling up at the stop. Funny there was a stop on this side of town. I assumed everyone on the East side could afford cars. I got back to the shelter right as the clock hands hit the half way mark.

"Where have you been?" Julie asked as I rushed from the front door to my room.

"Research."

"For your book?"

"Of course."

Part VI

I wasn't able to see Gaston the next day, nor the next. There was a job and education fair; Julie wanted to introduce me to a couple of people she knew at the university. She told them I was an aspiring author, full of ideas and notions. They smiled politely and said to bring them my story whenever it was ready. I told them I would.

The next day the weather was terrible. I begged Julie, the Director, the security guards, to let me go to the library. They said no. Severe storm warnings and flash flooding threatened. They told me to be thankful I had a warm, dry place to stay. Patted me on the head. Sent me on my way.

I had to see him. I felt something was cosmically wrong. No, not wrong, just shifting. Something was happening and I had to be a part of it. I knew if I got caught I'd be in big trouble. They could kick me out, send me to another shelter and I'd heard about those from some of the other ladies. But if I didn't go, I'd miss an altering. That was worth the risk.

I left Julie a note on my bed, just in case. I told her not to worry. I had to see a sick friend, confessed that's what I'd been doing with my time these days, going between him and the library. "Please don't kick me out," I signed it and eased down the hall toward the door that sometimes didn't latch. Luck! Someone had left it cracked. Running ahead of the approaching storm, I ducked into the church just as a patrol car rounded the corner. Eyes were everywhere and I was in no mood to be dragged back. I looked for the window with the dove and found it, polished back the grime from the brass plaque.

Edwin and Alice Lungstrom, 1765.

I smiled, traced their names. Edwin and Alice. Now I knew who to look for in the cemetery. Gaston's coughing stopped me cold. It was wet and terrible and I ran up the stairs.

He was in the middle of the room, trying to crawl to the broken window.

"What are you doing?"

"Gonna end it." He clawed at the floorboards.

"Don't be stupid. You'll just hurt yourself more."

He laughed and went into a fit of heaving. I held him until he calmed. "Impossible," he gasped.

"Are you out of water?"

He didn't answer and I pulled a fresh bottle from my jacket pocket. "Here," I opened it and poured some on his cracked lips. It ran down his neck, rolled off his soaked collar and down the broken buttons of his shirt.

"You were handsome once, weren't you?" I touched his forehead.

"Yes," a soft voice said. "Yes, he was."

Monica stood at the head of the steps. Gaston's body tensed and his breathing slowed to shallow, fearful gasps.

THE MYSTERIES OF DEATH AND LIFE

"He was glorious, Leah." She was dressed for mourning. She crossed the old bell tower and knelt beside us. "That's why I was terrified, you see, when I first saw him. My humanity frightened me and I was ashamed."

Gaston struggled to turn towards her. "Oh no! Don't you see? That's what makes you so beautiful! Your humanity, your flaws. I tired of perfection and you were golden light, shafts through broken glass."

I scooted out of the way and Monica took his face in her hands.

"Your friend paid me a visit," she stroked his brow. "Forced me to see things in a different light."

"She's crafty that way." He reached for me, found my hands.

"I'm ready to go," she whispered and Gaston stopped breathing.

"What?" I asked.

"I'm ready. You're right. Death isn't final. What we leave behind makes us live forever. I'm tired of trying to build something eternal. Tired of trying to etch my accomplishments in stone. Stone is cold and I don't want to be remembered for coldness." She pulled Gaston to his feet. "Come. Take me. I choose to go with you."

I stood and a soft breeze crossed my face. It didn't come from the busted windows but from Gaston. His emaciated body glowed crimson and I had to turn away from the light. When I looked back I cried and fell to my knees. He was whole again and looked at me with such gentleness I was afraid I might die.

"Not your time."

He lifted me to my feet and brushed back the hair from my eyes. His eyes sparkled, black as polished stone. His skin was moonlight, his hands felt like the water that gushed from the old rain gutters on the backside of the church, cool and cleansing. "But when it is, you will see me again." He knelt in front of me, put one of my hands to his face. "You saved me, Leah. You, the salvation of Death, rebuilt this mystery."

A hand appeared on his shoulder and I looked up at Monica. She shined like the stars on a clear, winter's night.

"Wait!" I cried out as they turned, as Gaston's black and silver wings brushed my face, the floor. "Wait! Don't leave me alone." I fell into sobs. "I don't want to be alone anymore."

I felt his breeze brush my cheeks. "You shall never be alone, Leah. Not with this," he touched my heart.

"But you'll be gone. I'll be alone. I'll have no one to…"

"Take care of?" He smiled and looked at Monica. "Oh, I think you'll have plenty to take care of. Besides, we're here," he touched my head and my heart. "What you do with us, is up to you."

And they were gone and I sat in the gathering puddles and cried.

Epilogue

Sunshine brushed my face. I sat up, got a head rush, lay down slowly. When the room stopped shifting, I turned and sat on the edge. I was in my own bed, barefoot and muddy. My face was tight along the trails of salt. I dusted as much mud off me as I could then shook out my shoes over the trash.

A knock on the door startled me. When I opened it Julie stood there with a stranger. He nodded with a smile; she looked as if she wanted to leap out of her skin.

"Leah, this is Mr. Applewhite. He says he has something to give you."

Confused, I followed them to Julie's office. Mr.

THE MYSTERIES OF DEATH AND LIFE

Applewhite opened his briefcase and handed me an envelope.

"My client was a very private person, Miss. A recluse most would say. I admit to being dumbfounded when this last minute request was made."

I held the envelope and turned it over, over, marveling at my name so elegant in black. The writing struck a chord. I tore into the envelope and extracted the paper within. It was smooth, more fabric than pulp, and the handwriting was as elegant as the woman had been. I sank in the chair, gasping. I shook my head and tried to form words but nothing came but a cross between a croak and a gurgle. I read the letter a second time, a third, and the words began to blur and the tears began to fall. Julie couldn't wait any longer and snatched it from my fingers.

She let out a stifled squeal, looked at me and asked. "How on earth did you 'make the acquaintance' of Monica Lungstrom?"

Making your acquaintance was the second greatest thing that ever happened to me in my long life.

"A mutual friend," I whispered and looked over the next two papers, these typewritten, not as lovely as the letter.

"'Left to Miss Leah Falstaff'...'Everything I own'... 'director of funds to restore the old church on East Cornwall'..." Julie read aloud. She looked at me and her eyes welled. She walked around the desk.

"Writing a story," she said and hugged me. "Why didn't you tell me you were helping out one of the richest people in the city?"

"But I..."

"Miss Lungstrom was very private," Mr. Applewhite repeated. "I'm sure she and Miss Falstaff had a mutual agreement of silence."

All I could do was nod.

We had no such agreement. I felt they wanted me

to tell their story, so I did. It was eventually published by Julie's acquaintances at the university. Thanks to Death's kindness, I was not only in charge of the restoration of the old Methodist church but also of the entire block that the shelter belongs to. That's why I now live at the address of the late Monica Lungstrom and why I am the caretaker of one of the largest eclectic book collections in the world.

And that's how Death saved me. Gaston said it was the other way around. All I did was talk some sense into a fallen angel. It was Death who gave me wings.

The End

Born and raised in the deep, dirty South, Jen Chandler cut her story-telling teeth in the old folktales of Appalachia. She grew up chasing ghosts and gods, devouring the myths and legends of Egypt, Greece, Ireland and the British Isles. Now happily ensconced beneath the moss laden oaks of Savannah, GA, Jen delights in rummaging into the dark corners of stories, re-imaging mythology and collecting ghosts, goblins, and other strange things that tap at the back door of her imagination. When not writing, Jen can be found drinking copious amounts of tea, designing and stitching fabric patterns, studying folk herbalism and re-reading old copies of British Country Living with frightening regularity. She may or may not be addicted to gummy candy.
Blog - Jen Chandler was Here: www.jenchandlerwashere.blogspot.com
Facebook: www.facebook.com/jen.chandler2
Instagram: www.instagram.com/jenchandlerwashere

The Silvering
by Ellen Jacobson

For the first time since childhood, a cool breeze caressed Caestu's right hand. Feeling the heavy, salty air on his skin, he shivered with pleasure. Pleasure that was tinged with fear. Fear of feeling something forbidden. Fear he would be discovered.

Pointing his fishing boat towards the harbor, he glanced at his hand resting on the wooden tiller. He rubbed his thumb along the crescent-shaped scar on his index finger, tracing the raised flesh, overwhelmed by the unfamiliar sensation, but unable to stop.

Caestu gripped the tiller tightly as the pleasure turned into pain. Again. It was happening again. He trembled as the muscles in his hand and arm tensed. The now familiar burn flowed from the center of his palm to his fingertips. His hand was silvering. A glove-like coating of molten silver crawled over his flesh, searing into the bones of his hand.

Caestu struggled to catch his breath. As the pain intensified, he looked at his scar and recalled how his mother had bandaged the cut as a child. "This should help ease the pain," she had said, as she applied salve onto his finger with a linen cloth. "Here, let me look at your hands. When did they get so big?" Her eyes had welled up with tears as she kissed his hands. "I can't believe this is the last time I'll see them."

Caestu closed his eyes tightly and muttered the Prayer of the Damned, trying to forget his mother's final touch before the gloving ceremony marking his tenth year. "Amani," he said, ending the prayer. Pressing his left thumb to his lips as a gesture of reverence, he grimaced as he felt the leather of his glove brush against his face. He opened his eyes, squinted in the bright sunlight and groaned.

Caestu wondered what his mother would do if she could see his right hand, ungloved and silvering. Would she stroke his hand until the silvering faded or would she push him away? She would choose the principles over him, he thought bitterly.

Caestu cringed in pain as he pulled his glove onto his silvering hand and pushed each finger into the harsh leather.

He tugged at the zipper on the wrist. Although the glove hid his silvered hand from sight, it seared and pulsed beneath the leather. The smell of burning flesh reminded him of that day two months ago when he broke with the principles and removed his glove for the first time.

A voice called out, jolting him back to the present. "You were foolish to try your luck over by Remorse Bay!" Caestu's heart raced as his friend, Guwante, steered his boat alongside and chuckled. "You should have come with us to Widow's Bay. Look at all of the *jarra* we caught! Show him, Piristine," Guwante said. He ruffled his son's hair while Piristine held up a reed basket full of the golden, spiny *jarra* that were a delicacy among the *kanni* caste.

They didn't see anything, Caestu reassured himself as he squeezed his gloved hands together. He reached over and grabbed the side of Guwante's boat, leaning in to admire their catch. "Let me have a look. You're becoming quite the fisherman, aren't you, Piristine?"

Guwante grinned. "No idle hands here. Let's have a look at your haul. Hmm, is that all you got? What happened? Nap on the beach again?"

Caestu looked down at the baskets in his boat. They might not be filled with *jarra*, but the purple shelled mollusks he netted would fetch a few coins at market. Enough to settle some debts and buy enough flagons of green ale to help him forget the silvering, for a while at least.

"Let's get our haul to market, Piristine." Guwante pushed off from Caestu's boat and raised his sails.

Caestu waved as their boat passed in front of his. "I'll see you at the Two Moons Tavern for evening meal," he shouted. "They might not serve *jarra*, but the eel stew isn't too bad if you wash it down with some green ale."

"Last one back to the wharf buys evening meal and plenty of that ale you're so fond of," Guwante taunted as his boat pulled ahead.

"I'd be a fool to take that bet!" Caestu yelled back. He frowned as he looked at his boat's patchwork sails, fraying lines and the rotting wood along the side of the hull. An ever-present bucket of tar was at hand to keep the worst of the leaks at bay. If only he had Guwante's boat instead; sleek and shiny with crisp sails, quick to respond and with ample room in the hold for *jarra* and other prized delicacies. Watching the wake of Guwante's boat as it surged ahead, Caestu resigned himself to the fact that the race was already lost.

At times, he wished he had Guwante's drive and ambition. Then maybe he would have a kindhearted wife at home. A wife wouldn't have let him stray from the principles. Caestu sighed. He'd already broken his vows. No woman would have him now if she knew what he had done.

The silvering on his hand faded as Caestu filled the sails with the eastern winds and tacked his boat into the harbor. He bit his lip as he watched the orange and purple colors ripple on the water while the sun began to set on the horizon. The silvering on his right hand now happened more frequently and took longer to fade each time. Would there come a time when his hand remained permanently silvered? There was no way to know. No one to ask. Secrets were concealed beneath gloves. Caestu held the tiller, whispering the words of the Prayer of the Damned as the winds pushed his boat towards the harbor.

* * *

As he tied his boat up, Caestu heard the conch shells blowing, announcing the presence of the *kanni*. People scurried out of the way as they entered the market. Although they engaged in ordinary tasks, such as shopping at the fish market, the *kanni* were anything but ordinary. In the early days, when the Others first arrived, they established the *kanni* caste, setting apart those considered superior in intellect and breeding. Upon the departure of the Others, the *kanni* were placed under the care and protection of the guardians. They only left their compound in groups, interacting with commoners under the watchful eyes of the guardians.

Caestu grabbed his baskets of mollusks and made his way down the creaking docks to the fish market. The fishmongers called out their wares.

"Get your eels here! Cleaned and ready for the pot!"

"Fresh and juicy *jarra*!"

"You won't find a better price on crayfish anywhere else!"

Caestu elbowed his way through the crowd and plopped his baskets down next to an old man shucking mollusks. Holding a knife in his thick rubber gloves, the old man pried open each purple shell and cut out the glistening meat. "What do you have for me today, Caestu?" he asked setting aside his knife and pulling off his rubber gloves, revealing a second pair of gloves made from canvas.

"I've got some mollusks. I reckon they're a lot

fresher and sweeter than those ones you're shucking there."

Rising from his stool, the old man eyed the baskets. "Hmm. Nothing special, but I guess they'll suffice," he said as he put a few coins in Caestu's outstretched hand.

Caestu continued to hold his hand out, staring at the old man until he dropped another into his palm. As he was closing the fingers of his red leather glove around the coins, Caestu felt his right hand tingle. It didn't feel like the burning sensation that preceded a silvering. More like the feeling of his mother tickling the palm of his hand when he was a child. He put the coins in his pocket. His eyes narrowed as he stared down at his glove and the tingling intensified.

The old man interrupted his thoughts. "Caestu, are you listening? You've been so absent-minded lately. I was asking if you've seen Guwante lately?"

"Sorry." Caestu looked up as he tried to ignore the sensation in his hand. "I saw Guwante out on the water today with his son, Piristine. They caught lots of *jarra*."

"You'd do well to follow Guwante's example. Focus more on your fishing and less on your daydreams." The old man emptied Caestu's baskets into a large wooden tub. "His boy should be coming of age and wearing gloves soon."

"Yes, he will be." Caestu hesitated for a moment. "Did you ever wonder what it would be like not to wear gloves?"

The old man sat on his stool and shook his head. "Not wear gloves? You really are dreaming foolish things these days. Off with you now. I've got work to do here," he said as he put his rubber gloves back on.

Caestu collected his baskets and walked back through the market. The tingling in his hand was growing stronger. His skin started to feel clammy. He struggled to breathe. He had the strange sensation that his hand was pulling him to someplace or someone.

He looked at the townspeople bargaining with the fishmongers, the guardians standing at attention with their conch shells held between their hands gloved in silk, the city wardens milling through the crowds, nudging people out of their way with their metal staffs, and the ungloved children playing and feeding scraps to the stray cats.

Then he saw her, inspecting the fresh *jarra* piled upon makeshift stands along the seawall. Her black robes fluttered in the eastern winds as she picked up the plump *jarras* with her delicate gloved hands and placed them in her basket. He broke out into a cold sweat as his hand pulsated. Was this who his hand was drawing him to?

A dark blue, silk sash cinched her robes, marking her as *kanni*. It was forbidden to speak to her without permission. Even approaching her involved risk, but he had to know who she was. The stares of the guardians burned into him as he walked towards the stands. He bent over the piles of *jarra* on display, inspecting them, as though searching for the freshest ones.

She edged towards him and placed her right hand on his arm. A burning heat came through her black glove, seeping through the dense felt of his jacket. Not daring to meet her eyes, he studied the dark blue triangles embroidered on her glove instead. He felt faint as she drew nearer and the heat grew stronger.

"I know what you are," she whispered as she tightened her grip on his arm. "I know what you've done."

The conch shells sounded. She removed her gloved hand from his arm. He looked up and found her staring at him with piercing green eyes, eyes the color of the seas. He averted his gaze while she turned to join the procession of *kanni* making their way from the fish market back onto the main thoroughfare.

* * *

"How old are you now, Piristine?" asked Caestu as he grabbed his flagon of green ale.

"I'll be of age next month," he answered, plucking a piece of eel from his stew and licking the grease off his bare hands.

"Now mind your manners, son," said Guwante. "Don't be picking food out of your bowl like that. You're going to be gloved soon. It's time you stopped acting like a child." Guwante turned to Caestu. "You'll be expected at the gloving ceremony and celebration."

Piristine tugged at Caestu's arm. "There'll be cakes and sherbets and my mother is even going to make some of those almond pastries. You have to come!"

"Of course I'll be there. You know I have a weakness for your mother's almond pastries." Caestu winked. "I wouldn't miss those for anything."

Caestu pulled his bowl towards him and speared a piece of eel with a heavy, bronze fork. "Enjoy your freedom while you can, Piristine. Once you don your gloves, you'll never feel things like that piece of eel you're holding in your hands again."

"Freedom?" Guwante scoffed as he tore off a chunk of dark bread and shook his head. "Bare hands aren't freedom. They're a mark of childhood. Of immaturity. Of weakness. When the Others came, they taught us the principles. They taught us to cover our hands." His voice grew more strident as he pointed at Caestu's gloves. "These remind us that some things aren't meant for us. We don't defile things with our hands. We don't take pleasure in feeling things with our hands."

Piristine looked at his father for a few moments and then blurted out, "I heard mother say there are some villages across the seas where people don't wear gloves. They touch things with their bare hands!" He pulled back when he saw the look on his father's face.

Guwante slammed his cup down on the table. "Nonsense! Did your mother fill your head with these kinds of fairy tales, Caestu?"

Caestu stared down at his gloves. "No. Following the principles was important to her." He looked up at Piristine, his face etched with bittersweet memories. "I remember how proud she was of me at my gloving ceremony, just like your mother will be."

Piristine smiled and dug back into his stew. Guwante tapped his fingers on the table and glowered while Caestu drank the rest of his ale.

"What do you think the Others look like?" Piristine asked as he fished out another piece of eel from his bowl.

Guwante stroked his beard while he thought about Piristine's question. "Once, when I was a boy, I saw one of the ancient texts on a pilgrimage. There was an illustration of the Others holding up silver hands. The priest told us they wore gloves made of silver," Guwante said. "Now, enough about the Others. Ours is not to question, isn't that right?" he asked, staring at his son. Piristine nodded as he looked down at his bare hands.

Caestu shivered as he looked down at his own gloved hands.

* * *

Caestu stumbled out of the tavern and made his way through the crooked alleyways to his lodgings. Both moons were large, their light casting a deep red glow on the uneven cobblestones. Blood moons were rare, a reminder of the day, long ago, when the Others first came.

The moonlight brought his thoughts back to his own ceremony when his mother had presented him with red leather gloves. "The faithful wear gloves of this color to remind themselves of the principles," she had told him. Even after her passing, he still wore red gloves. Not to remind him of the principles, but to remind him of her.

As he went to unlock the doorway to his lodgings, his hand started to tingle again, like it had earlier in the market with the *kanni*. He almost dropped his key as he felt her presence behind him.

"Quickly, open up the door before anyone sees us," she said.

Caestu nodded, turned the key and held open the large wooden door. He motioned for her to enter first as he looked down at the chipped tiled floor of the hallway. He jumped back as a large, hooded figure followed behind her.

She lifted up her black robes and stepped over the threshold. "You may call me Remsamdi. And what may I call you?" she asked once they were inside. When he didn't reply, she turned to him impatiently. "You may speak. I'm here in your lodgings without guardians. Do you really think we should be standing on ceremony? What's your name?"

"Caestu," he stammered. "My name is Caestu."

"Good. A strong name. You'll need strength in the coming days." She peered down the hallway. "Now, which are your rooms?"

Caestu led her to a door with flying fish carved into the dark green wood. His hands shook as he opened the door. "Please, my lady, I apologize. My lodgings are simple. Not worthy of *kanni*." He bowed his head as she brushed past him.

Remsamdi looked around the sitting room with its dark brown plastered walls and high ceiling. She touched the woven blanket covering the settee with her gloved hand, rubbing the material between her fingertips. Her gloves are so delicate, Caestu thought.

He wondered if she could feel the soft mohair of the blanket through them. No, he reminded himself. Gloves were meant to protect their wearers from temptations, even the finely crafted gloves of *kanni.*

Remsamdi walked over to the small wooden table in the corner, pulled out one of the rickety chairs and sat while her companion stood behind her, hidden from view beneath the dark hood. Remsamdi looked at Caestu coldly for a few moments. "You offer no refreshment?"

He face heated. "My apologies, my lady. Please, allow me get you something to drink."

Caestu went into the cooking alcove and rummaged through the cupboards looking for something suitable to serve to the *kanni.* The cupboards were bare, save for some ice brandy. He leaned against the counter and covered his face with his hands.

"Caestu, we're waiting." The tone of her voice made his blood run cold. He grabbed the brandy and hurried into the sitting room.

"My lady, may I ask a question?" Caestu poured brandy into enamel cups, grimacing as he spilled some on the tablecloth. Remsamdi gave a slight nod. He took a deep breath and straightened his shoulders. "At the fish market, you said that you knew what I was, what I had done. What did you mean by that?" Realizing how bold he had been, Caestu slumped into his chair and started to shake.

Remsamdi eyed him as he passed one of the cups to her. After taking a cautious sip, she said, "Perhaps it would be simpler if I just showed you."

Caestu gasped as Remsamdi unzipped her right glove and pulled it off her hand. He knew he should avert his eyes, but he couldn't. He was captivated by the sight of her removing her glove. The only hands he ever saw were those of children too young to be gloved, like Piristine. The thought of seeing the

THE SILVERING

hand of an adult, especially that of a *kanni*, terrified him. His mouth hung open in shock as she finished removing her glove. Her hand was starting to silver. Just like his did.

"But, how..." he stammered. "Why is your hand silvering?" He grabbed his cup and felt the ice brandy burn his throat as he gulped it down. He wiped his mouth on his sleeve and twisted his hands together. Summoning his courage, he asked, "Please, my lady, tell me. Why is your hand silvering?"

She stared icily at him. "You already know the answer to that, don't you, Caestu? I removed my right glove and touched something with my bare hand. Just like you did. Now, show me your hand. I know the truth, otherwise I wouldn't be here."

Caestu looked down at his red leather gloves. Could he show someone else his hand? Could he show her, a *kanni*, his hand? He glanced at the figure looming behind her.

"Ignore him and do as I say," she commanded.

As he debated with himself, Caestu felt the burning start in his hand. Looking over at her silvered hand resting on the table, he took a deep breath and tugged at the zipper on his right glove. He pulled it partway down and hesitated as the pain seared through his hand.

"Give me your hand," she said. She pulled the zipper all the way down and removed his glove. As his hand came into contact with the cool night air, the silvering reached his fingertips. He looked down at his hand and then raised his eyes to meet hers for a brief moment.

"Now tell me what happened," she ordered.

He looked at his hand as though it was the first time he had seen it silvering. "Two months ago, I took my boat to the Isle of Rothriki. If you walk through the woods, there's a small cave where they say the

HERO LOST: MYSTERIES OF DEATH AND LIFE

Others sheltered when they first came here. There was a big storm that day, so I went inside to wait until the weather cleared. Towards the back of the cave there's a stone ledge with a pile of sacred bones on it."

He paused and looked back down at her hand. Her silvering had started to fade. He noticed the smoothness of her skin. No scars or imperfections, unlike his own.

"I know the place," she said, pulling her hand away from his gaze. "I went there as a young girl on a pilgrimage. All around the ledge are signs warning pilgrims not to disturb the bones. Did you heed the warnings, Caestu?" she asked.

He glanced at her with a hint of defiance in his eyes. "No, I didn't. I needed to touch the bones. Not with my gloved hand, but to feel them between my bare fingers. It was a sensation that..." Caestu hesitated, trying to find the right words for something that he couldn't explain. "I don't know how to describe it," he said finally.

Caestu started to reach for his cup with his bare right hand. Realizing what he was doing, he grabbed it with his gloved left hand instead and gulped the brandy down. "I didn't have a choice. I had to touch them," he said with a strangled voice.

"Yes, Caestu. I know that desire," Remsamdi said. "I first felt it when I was studying at the temple. I would spend my afternoons in the Hall of Wisdom, sifting through the dusty tomes."

She shifted in her seat and looked down at the table. "One day, I was looking at a manuscript about early encounters with the Others. I found a passage describing what happened to the first people who met the Others. There was an illustration at the top of the page of a dark black eye with a ring of fire in its center. The symbol of the Others."

"My mother used to wear a tiny fire eye on a gold

bracelet," Caestu said as he gazed out the window at the blood red moons. "She said it protected her from harm."

"I was drawn to the eye. I felt compelled to touch it. I took off my right glove and traced my fingers over the eye." Remsamdi's eyes narrowed. "I could feel the heat of the ring of fire on my fingertips."

Remsamdi sat back in her chair, slipped her glove back onto her right hand and pulled the zipper up. "Since that day, my hand, like yours, began silvering."

Caestu listened to the steady tick tock of the clock. The sound grew louder and louder as questions tangled up in his head. Finally, the words came out as Caestu gripped the edge of the table, oblivious to the fact that he was tearing the lace tablecloth. "I don't understand. Why is this happening to me? To you? Is this a curse from the Others? Is this because I broke the principles?"

Remsamdi turned to her companion. He stepped forward and pulled back his hood. "We are those to whom you refer as the Others," he said in a low voice. Caestu willed himself to look up. He drew back in his chair and gasped. He found himself staring into inky black eyes, eyes as dark as the onyx stones worn by the priests. Eyes blazing with a red ring of fire in the center.

"We *are* the Others," the man repeated.

"You're one of them," Caestu said faintly.

"I am. As is Remsamdi. As are you. You're one of us. You're one of the Others," he said, his deep voice reverberating across the slate floor.

Caestu struggled to take it all in. He gloved his right hand and rose from his chair. He cleared the brandy and cups off the table and escaped into the kitchen alcove. As he put everything on the counter, he glanced at the portrait on the wall. His mother, with her red gloved hands primly folded in her lap, and a boy with curly black hair standing next to her, grinning and holding a pair of new red leather gloves in his bare hands. His gloving ceremony. She became ill soon after that day, he thought sadly.

Remsamdi walked up behind him. "There are things you must know. Come." She motioned him back into the sitting room.

"You have two choices, Caestu," Remsamdi said as they sat down at the table. "You can stay here and continue to live your life as you have, as though you have no secrets to hide. Work hard, marry, have children, see your children gloved. Live a simple life alongside your friends and neighbors." She paused. "For a time, at least. Or, you can cast away your gloves and leave the city."

Caestu's eyes grew wide. "Leave the city? Why? Where would I go?"

"Across the seas. Dorez will take you," she said, nodding at the tall, cloaked figure. "You will go with him and be with those who are like you. Others who also experience the silvering."

Caestu jumped as conch shells sounded outside his window. He went to the window and peered out. "How strange. It's the guardians, but there aren't any *kanni* with them. They seem to be searching for something."

"Or searching for someone," Remsamdi said as she and Dorez exchanged glances.

Caestu turned away from the window. "Would you leave the city as well, my lady?"

Dorez replied instead. "Remsamdi may not travel across the seas. She is *kanni*. She is barred from leaving."

"I don't understand," Caestu said looking at Remsamdi. "You are *kanni*. You are the highest among us. You can do what you want."

Remsamdi's expression soured. "You think the

kanni are special?" she asked, spitting out her words. "The *kanni* don't have any freedom. The guardians aren't there to *protect* us. They're there to *watch* us. Who do you think the guardians are looking for? They're looking for me. To take me to the compound and put me back in my gilded cage."

Remsamdi stood and paced back and forth. "The *kanni* are born with a natural curiosity. As children, they're inquisitive, they wonder how things work, they challenge. The guardians stifle their thirst for knowledge, but they can't quench it completely. The *kanni* are the descendants of the Others. We give into temptation, remove our gloves and become marked with silver. Like you. You have the blood of the Others in you."

Caestu thought about what Remsamdi said as he stared out the window at the guardians. "But, how can you be one of the Others? How can I be one of the Others?" He turned and pointed at Dorez. "The Others have fire in their eyes. Like him."

"Have you ever seen an old *kanni*?" Remsamdi asked. "Their eyes change when they become older. Once they do, the guardians never let them out of the compound again."

Caestu studied Dorez. Long, gray hair framed his deeply lined face. Caestu looked from Dorez to Remsamdi in disbelief.

Dorez moved closer to Remsamdi. "The *kanni* cannot come with us. The guardians would hunt her down. She must stay."

Remsamdi leaned forward. "But you can leave. The guardians don't know that occasionally a commoner is born with the same curiosity as the *kanni*. A curiosity which overwhelms them, which compels them to remove their gloves and touch what is forbidden. Dorez and I find them, like we found you, and offer them a choice. Stay and conceal your silvering, knowing that eventually your eyes will change. Or go across the seas."

"Does anyone stay?" Caestu asked. "If I stayed, what would happen when my eyes changed?"

"Only a few have ever stayed. We watch them. When the time comes for their eyes to change, well, they know what they have to do," Remsamdi said. "They know what would happen if they were discovered."

Caestu's eyes grew wide. Could she mean what he thought she meant? "Are you saying they…" his voice trailed off, unable to bring himself to say the words.

Remsamdi shrugged her shoulders. "Yes, they sacrifice themselves. But by that time, they've had a full life. It's the price they pay for hiding their silvering and living like others do. Is that what you want, Caestu? A normal life?"

Caestu thought about how his mother's eyes had lit up when she talked about having grandchildren one day, teaching them the principles and watching them be gloved. Then he thought about the cool breeze blowing on his bare hand while sailing his boat.

"But the principles, the Others came to give us the principles." Caestu rubbed his temples, trying to reconcile what Remsamdi was telling him with what he had learned from his mother and the priests.

"The Others never came to give us the principles. There never were any principles to begin with," Remsamdi said angrily. "The guardians and the priests are not who you think they are. They twisted everything. They rounded us up, branded us as *kanni* and set us apart. They created the principles, rules devised to control all of us, wrapped up in mythical origins and presented as scripture.

"Do you know what this really means?" Remsamdi pressed her left thumb to her lips as though she was ending a prayer. "This is a reminder to *kanni* not to speak of their origins. To stay silent. That's why we

THE SILVERING

find people like you, commoners who are silvering. Once there are enough of you, you can speak. You can speak for all of us. You will cross the seas with Dorez," she said, as though the matter was settled.

Caestu thought back to Piristine's questions over evening meal. His wonder at the possibility of people who didn't wear gloves. Would he become one of the silvered who Remsamdi would sense one day?

"Come, we must go," Remsamdi said to Dorez. As she walked towards the door, she cautioned Caestu. "When your hand starts silvering, be careful not to draw attention to yourself. Ignore the burning, act like nothing is happening. Don't give the guardians a reason to suspect that commoners experience silvering. They're watching. They're always watching."

Her green eyes grew cold. "You have much to reflect on, Caestu, but not much time to do so. You and Dorez must cross the seas soon before the winds shift to the west."

* * *

After a sleepless night, Caestu left his lodgings in search of bread and cheese for his midday meal. As he made his way down the main thoroughfare into the town square, he heard the sound of conch shells. He stepped aside as the *kanni* marched in single file, their dark blue sashes trailing behind them. The *kanni* halted as the guardians formed a circle around them. One by one each of the *kanni* turned to go into the various shops lining the square.

Caestu saw Remsamdi as she stepped in front of one of the guardians, her head held high, her green eyes staring straight ahead. As she walked past him, holding her basket at her side, he looked down at the pavement. Out of the corner of his eye, he saw one of the guardians come towards her.

"*Kanni*, you look unwell. Let me see your eyes," the guardian said as he tilted her head up. "Yes, your eyes are getting darker."

She gripped her basket in her hands as she tried to pull away. "You're mistaken. There's nothing wrong with them."

The guardian pulled her to him, digging his thumb into the palm of her gloved hand.

A crowd started to gather around Remsamdi and the guardian. Caestu heard them murmuring that they had never seen a guardian treat a *kanni* this way.

"Why is your hand burning, *kanni*? I can feel it through your glove," the guardian growled. "It's happening, isn't it?" he asked.

Remsamdi twisted and pulled her hand away. "Yes, it's happening. My hand is silvering." She unzipped her glove. The guardian tried to stop her. She pushed him sharply. He stumbled backwards, falling onto the ground. She ripped off her glove, holding her hand high for all to see.

Silver. Molten silver. Her fingers shimmered. The crowd gasped. She turned and stared at Caestu, holding his gaze as her green eyes turned to black. He thought of his mother's old fire eye bracelet as a ring of fire started burning in the center of each of her darkened eyes.

The guardian got to his feet and grabbed Remsamdi. As he forced her glove back on her hand, she shouted to the crowd, "What secrets do your gloves hide? What secrets do your neighbors' gloves hide?" She pointed to the other guardians rushing over. "Ask yourselves, what secrets are they concealing from you?"

As the guardians led Remsamdi away forcibly, they reassured the crowd, "This *kanni* is unwell. She's delirious. She doesn't know what she's saying. Go about your business."

Caestu saw Guwante and Piristine on the other side of the square, Piristine's eyes wide with wonder.

THE SILVERING

Piristine tugged at his father's sleeve. Guwante knelt down next to him, whispering something in his ear. The boy stared at Remsamdi as she was led away.

Caestu listened to the sound of the conch shells fading off in the distance. He watched as the crowd dispersed. The merchants went back into their shops and people hurried down the alleyways. Caestu turned and walked towards the wharf.

* * *

Caestu found Dorez waiting for him at the wharf, his cloak wrapped tightly around him and his hood drawn low over his face.

"Well, have you decided?" Dorez asked. When Caestu hesitated, he growled. "You saw what happened to the *kanni*. You have no choice."

Caestu drew in a deep breath, nodded and motioned for Dorez to climb into his boat. As Caestu tossed his bags into the hold, Piristine ran up to him holding a pair of pale yellow gloves.

"Did you see what happened on the square?" the boy asked, his eyes bright with excitement. Piristine looked back at his father glaring at him. "Never mind, we aren't supposed to talk about it."

"That's probably for the best," Caestu said as he looked at the gloves Piristine held in his hands.

"Father bought these for my gloving ceremony." Piristine stroked the gloves with his bare hands. "They feel so soft, like the mohair blanket my mother made for me."

Caestu felt a lump in his throat. "My mother made a blanket like that for me once." He looked out across the harbor at the rocky islands dotting the seas. "I don't remember what it felt like anymore." He ran his hand along the boy's cheek and smiled. "Don't let your gloves take your memories away from you." Caestu sighed and pointed at Dorez. "This man hired me to take him to the Outer Islands, so I'll be gone for a while."

Piristine looked puzzled as he helped Caestu untie his lines and push his boat off of the dock. He waved goodbye with his new gloves clutched in his hand as Caestu's boat floated out of sight. Caestu filled the sails with the eastern winds and pointed his boat towards the lands across the seas. Then he turned to Dorez, removed his glove, reached out and tentatively clasped Dorez's hand with his own, silver touching silver.

The End

Ellen Jacobson writes mystery and sci-fi/fantasy stories. She is currently working on the first in a cozy mystery series about a reluctant sailor turned amateur sleuth, as well as tales set on imaginary worlds. She lives on a sailboat with her husband, exploring the world from the water. When she isn't working on boat projects or seeking out deserted islands, she blogs about their adventures at The Cynical Sailor - www.thecynicalsailor.blogspot.com
You can also find her on *Facebook* - www.facebook.com/TheCynicalSailor/

Memoirs of a Forgotten Knight
By Renee Cheung

There were pockets of the Web that few have visited. Outdated, irrelevant content or failed experiments made for unpopular websites. The server spaces these sites lived in lay fallow and unattended like the lonely wilderness of abandoned lands. Or at least abandoned by humans. As with those places in the Physical, inhabitants of another sort came to lay claim. Protected by humankind's neglect, the Unseen that migrated to the Digital came to these deserted bits of server memory, making them their home across scattered networks.

The dragon was one such being. Nestled in a dim, empty folder, buried several levels deep, it curled into itself. Ebony walls of the metaphorical cave were streaked with patterned gold, once glistening but now dulled by disuse. Occasionally, the lair pulsed as if yearning for attention, but those moments were fleeting. In contrast, the large creature itself glowed with the vitality of life in the Digital; its scales a green hue that shimmered and sparkled. Great, emerald orbs would cast around and look satisfactorily upon its home.

Mostly, however, the dragon slept, overlooked by even others of its kind. Resting in a nest made of fragmented files, gold and coppery sheaves of paper, the dragon dreamed. It remembered another time forgotten by most. It was a time before the Great Migration. It was a time before the Unseen became the Unseen.

* * *

HERO LOST: MYSTERIES OF DEATH AND LIFE

"Please, Sir Knight, please, you have to help us!" The village elder, bent with age, hastened to approach the knight. His grey beard quivered with each syllable. The elder's daughter accompanied her father, supporting the old man on one side. She was pleasing to look at, with white-blond locks and cheeks pinked from the cold.

Cormac was in the process of stabling his horse when the elder, along with a group of villagers, came pleading. But he had already known what the villagers were going to ask, for it was what brought him there in the first place. The rumour of a dragon to be slain was not one any knight worth his salt could ignore. And although Cormac was little more than a hedge knight, lordless for the time being, he was still a knight, sworn to defend those that could not do so themselves.

Cormac finished tying off the reins then turned and stood a little taller, attempting to look reassuring, when really, all he wanted was to sit down and shake off the travel dust. At least the village elder had recognized him as a knight. Despite the armour he wore, Cormac was more lanky than lean, and his youthful, beardless face often contradicted the depth of experience he actually had. As a result, Cormac had always struggled to effect the commanding presence of a knight. Still, he always tried and so, he nodded gravely. "The dragon, of course. It is what I am here for."

Anxious expressions turned into cautious relief, and there were even a few hesitant smiles. There may be those skeptical of the young knight but if so, desperation had made them eager to believe that their hero had arrived, and even more eager to help said hero. The village elder nodded back at Cormac as his daughter looked at the knight with new respect and admiration. It was a look that Cormac hoped he could earn. "Is there a place where we may sit and talk? I would learn all I can about this dragon before I take action."

"That is wise," the village elder replied, appearing to be calmer now that Cormac had accepted the task. "Let us adjourn to the tavern. We can talk there."

"And perhaps Sir Knight would care for some food and drink as well?" The daughter favoured Cormac with a gentle smile.

"Ah, yes, food and drink. You must be weary from your travels. Forgive my lack of manners. The dragon and the havoc it's been wreaking have been all I can think about as of late," the elder bemoaned.

"No harm done. I understand," Cormac replied and gestured for them to lead the way.

Much of the village laid in ruins. Remnants of destroyed buildings still smoldered like dying embers. A young woman, surrounded by small children wailing their fears, wept over a plot of newly turned earth. Here and there, a building would remain standing, yet even those showed signs of damage—a missing roof, a collapsed side, charred walls. The scent of blood and fire permeated the air. Yet the villagers toiled. As Cormac was escorted towards the tavern, he saw a group of men grimly digging through rubble and neatly piling it into heaps. Two women sat on the steps of a house that no longer existed, chattering away while they worked on their sewing.

The tavern itself remained mostly intact, and repairs were well on their way with a roof half-thatched. Inside, it was little more than one large room with a doorway to one side that led to the kitchen. Next to it, an old wooden bar spanned lengthwise. On the opposite side, a large fireplace stood cold and unattended. Tables and chairs were scattered across the space in between. As they entered, the smell of roasted meat and old ale greeted them, and Cormac's stomach immediately growled. The knight coughed, covering up the sound, and relaxed a little when it appeared that no one noticed. The elder led him to a table directly in the middle of the room, and the rest of the villagers settled around them.

"The dragon, you see, only began appearing in the last few months," the elder began as the barkeep, a burly but not unkind looking man, brought over a bowl of stew that was accompanied by a tankard. Only the best for their would-be saviour, or so Cormac hoped, then immediately felt guilty for thinking so. Although he was intent on consuming the meal before him, he paid close attention to all that was said. Sometimes information was all the power needed to tip the scales in battle.

"The dragon comes down occasionally to burn and ravage. Never completely destroys everything, though. Surely it could if it wanted to. There seems to be no rhyme or reason as to why it comes. It certainly doesn't take food every time. We tried talking to it when it first appeared, but it didn't seem to understand language. We've even tried to leave it a sacrifice, but that didn't work either."

"A maiden?" Cormac abruptly looked up from his food at the elder. He had to ask, even though he wasn't sure what he would do if the elder confirmed it. The act of sacrificing a human life was barbaric, no matter how desperate the situation. Cormac frowned and scanned for signs of guilt in the small crowd that gathered around them, but found none.

"A cow," the elder replied, stiffening. He tilted his chin upwards and sniffed, but after a moment, he sighed.

Cormac released the tension in his body.

"It's living up in the mountain behind the village. It's an old mountain, and there are trails we used before the dragon arrived. There is a cave that it makes its home in," another villager interjected.

"There was another knight that went up the mountain three days ago. An older fellow. He came in here claiming he had killed countless dragons before. I mean, he certainly looked the part with his golden armour and all, but we haven't heard from him since." The barkeep pulled a chair alongside the table.

"Was there a dragon insignia on his armour?" Cormac's voice remained calm, but he pursed his lips. If this was indeed who he thought it was, then this dragon was even more dangerous than expected. The Dragon Slayer was reputed to be one of the fiercest knights, specializing in fearsome creatures. With all the rumours of a dragon travelling from place to place to attack different villages circulating, Cormac supposed he shouldn't be surprised that the famous knight would have come here. But if the Dragon Slayer did not return...

"Aye." The elder watched Cormac closely.

The old man was not the only one. Cormac could feel the other villagers' eyes on him, judging, sizing him up, and comparing him to the other knight. He swallowed once and sucked in a breath. He needed more information.

"Anything you can tell me about the dragon's appearance? Size?"

"I'd say it's about two or three times this tavern. Its wings span wider, though. Green lizard, this one."

"Here," the elder's daughter took something out of her pocket and handed it to Cormac. It was a single dragon scale, an iridescent green emerald, glistening even in the dim, tavern light. As hard as metal, it gave off a ting when Cormac tapped it lightly against his bowl. "I picked it up after the last attack."

"It had the bluest eyes," another said softly. "It was the second attack. It stared right at me. I thought I was going to die, but then it flew away."

"I saw it, too, but it had brown eyes, not blue!" another exclaimed.

"Are you all sure this is one dragon we are talking about here?" Cormac asked sharply. He looked from one villager to another, studying both of the speakers. Dragons usually only gathered for coupling and then would part ways. Rarely did they remain together for they were too territorial. Or so his research had said. Perhaps fear had addled their memories.

"Aye, it has to be. The same green and the same mad terror," the elder replied with a frown on his lips. "One of our boys snuck up to spy on the dragon. Brave but foolish lad. But he did confirm that it was only one dragon."

Silent in his thoughts, Cormac nodded. The colour of the creature's eyes hardly mattered when dragon slaying, but he would keep in mind to confirm that there was only one dragon before taking action. Best be sure than to happen upon a rude surprise.

"Wicked claws and wicked breath," the elder muttered, and then looked up at Cormac. "We do not ask you to risk your life for nothing. We have been fortunate in trade, and our village has put together a decent reward." He paused and leaned forward. "So, will you go, Sir Knight?"

"I'll set off in the morning," Cormac replied. Today, he would interview other witnesses and rest while he could. Tomorrow, at the very least, he would verify the villagers' accounts with his own two eyes. But if the opportunity to do more arose, he would do what he could.

* * *

It was another lovely day. The morning dew had frosted the path with tiny crystals. The cool air nipped at Cormac's fingers, and the winter sun did little to warm him up as he made his way up the mountain. It was an ancient one with many of its slopes gentled by time, while its surface was scarred by numerous paths and game trails. Evergreens gently swayed, part of the lush, vibrant forest that grew from fertile soil. There was peace here, despite the threat ahead.

Unlike the Dragon Slayer, he chose to wear no armour. He had traded protection for maneuverability after hearing one witness tell of how quick the dragon was. Besides, no amount of iron could possibly protect him from the dragon's fiery breath. Still, many had looked upon Cormac that morning as he set off with doubt written clearly on their faces.

The villagers' directions pointed him true. As he climbed higher, he noticed that taller trees became sparser and the sounds of the forest faded, leaving an eerie silence. At times, he found patches of scorched earth. Tracking those signs, he arrived at the dragon's lair.

It was just as described. The cave cut into precipitous slopes, gray rocks streaked with brown. A clearing of dried dirt spread out before its entrance like a welcome mat, although the invitation was hardly a warm one. Menacing shadows cast odd shapes against the debris that littered the ground. The remains of a cart. A piece of tattered cloth. Yet, there were no human bones nor armour in sight, which was a curiosity in itself. The only bones Cormac could see were that of livestock. Had the Dragon Slayer even been here?

The knight hid behind a small clump of bushes that grew stubbornly next to the mouth of the cave and tried his best to discern any details about its interior. But the darkness only deepened such that Cormac could see little beyond the first few feet. He waited, hoping for a chance to catch a glimpse of the dragon outside where he had more visibility. In truth, Cormac did not want to take action until he was sure he had the facts straight.

HERO LOST: MYSTERIES OF DEATH AND LIFE

But it was to no avail. Hours passed, and yet there was still no sign of the dragon. If he waited any longer, the day's efforts would have been for naught. He pursed his lips, debating whether to enter the cave. Perhaps the dragon was not home, or perhaps it was in there, with no plans of emerging. Frozen by doubt, it took a while longer before he finally decided. The knight pushed his misgivings to the back of his mind and reluctantly left the safety of his hiding spot. If he was able to catch the dragon unaware, he reasoned, he could slay it in its sleep. So, with trepidation dragging his heels, Cormac crept slowly towards the cave, and entered.

Inside, the dank air hung almost unnaturally still, and there were no other signs of life. The walls were moist, and the sound of trickling water echoed through the chamber; evidence of a source somewhere deeper. Cormac waited until his eyes adjusted to the darkness and he could make out more of the cave. The first chamber was unexpectedly small, but it appeared that a tunnel on the far end led deeper into a second cavern. Hugging the walls, he moved cautiously onwards, careful to not unsettle any debris or make more noise than he could help. His footsteps, as soft as they were, already felt loud enough.

Following the sonorous sound of snoring, punctuated occasionally with a snuff, he entered the second chamber, a much larger one appropriate for a dragon. Here, weak sunlight filtered through from above, and dust motes danced in the air. But the blackness swallowed the light before it reached further into the cave, and beneath, shrouded in darkened shadows laid a large silhouette, curled in the center.

The dragon slumbered in a deep sleep. As Cormac studied the cavern, he noted a single body slumped against the wall. Gingerly, he made his way there and knelt down on the cold floor. A strapping lad, no more than eighteen, gazed ahead with empty, lifeless eyes. Blood, which once soaked the leather from a single stab wound to the stomach, now left only a large rust coloured stain. It was a wound more likely inflicted by a sword than a claw, and this disturbed Cormac greatly. The knight looked up and scanned the cavern once more. No other corpses, nor golden armour, were in sight. This must be the result of some sort of foul play. Regardless of what happened, however, there were more pressing matters at hand.

Leaving the corpse for the moment, Cormac crept closer to the dragon, growing more daring as it did not stir. The dragon's tail, long and sinewy, wrapped around a powerful body that rose and fell in great heaves with every breath. Prismatic scales with an iridescent sheen glittered against the murkiness, appearing to shine without aid. But in contrast to the almost beautiful sight, the air reeked of rotten eggs and burnt meat. It was nearly enough to make Cormac lose his stomach, but the knight steeled himself. At least the chamber was comfortably warm, so much that Cormac was grateful for his decision to forgo his armour. Taking an even closer look at the dragon, his eyes sought any weakness.

Suddenly, without warning, the dragon snorted, and its tail unfurled to sweep across the dusty floor. Its eyes snapped open, revealing sapphires that illuminated the cavern. A forked tongue darted between wicked fangs as the dragon's mouth opened wide in a yawn. Cormac held his breath and remained as still as he possibly could. His heart pounded. Finally, much to his relief, the dragon's tail curled back around its body, and the reptilian eyelids closed once more.

That moment was enough. Just as in tales of old, Cormac had caught a glimpse of the dragon's one vulnerability. Beneath the hard scales of its body laid a soft belly, one that would not give any resistance to a sword's edge. Although it was nearly impossible to reach, it was still his best chance to end the creature. With that in mind, Cormac retreated to a clump of rocks and settled behind them to think through the best approach.

He noted that the dragon seemed to be aware of its Achilles' heel, as it slept curled up, limiting access to that soft part. That made slaying the dragon in its sleep less of an option. On the other hand, it was hard to develop any sort of tactics for slaying an awake dragon when he had only ever seen it sleep. In the back of his mind, Cormac could hear the old knight he was apprenticed to chastising him.

Most younglings have issues with being too hot-headed but yeesh, Cormac, you are just the opposite. Stop overthinking everything. In the heat of the battle, sometimes one must go with one's instincts. If you keep second-guessing yourself, one day you will find a sword in you before you can even reason yourself into action.

Cormac shook his head clear. Now was not the time to be recalling old memories. His mind turned the problem over and over, marveling at it like a theoretical puzzle. It was something he often did when stumped. He peeked over the rocks once more to check on the dragon. Only, it was no longer there. Swearing inwardly, he adjusted himself into a crouch and scanned the cavern, trying to ascertain where it went. He was still searching when the foul stench grew stronger and a gust of dank breath nearly knocked him off his feet. Just as the dragon's mouth clamped down on where he was hidden, he rolled instinctively out of the way and drew his sword in one fluid motion.

The dragon roared in frustration. The sound thundered across the chamber and rattled the knight.

MEMOIRS OF A FORGOTTEN KNIGHT

The time for thinking and planning was over. Cormac scrambled to his feet and lengthened the distance between himself and the dragon. The wings and tail could easily be his downfall as much as the dragon's teeth and breath.

A jet of fire shot towards him. He deftly darted out of the way.

A still target was a dead target. Cormac danced across the cavern, making himself as difficult a target as he could. He subtly moved closer to the dragon, every movement fighting against the instinct that screamed at him to run away. The closer he was, the harder it would be for the creature to attack with its short forearms, eliminating one potential threat.

Unfortunately, Cormac hadn't accounted for the long, flexible neck. As the dragon pivoted once more, its sharp teeth snapped at Cormac, nearly catching him by the shoulder. The knight dodged just in time, and then saw his chance. There was a second of hesitation, but he took a deep breath and pushed through. It was all or nothing, and nothing meant his life.

He ran faster than he had ever run in his life, keeping low as he ducked beneath the dragon's body in what was surely a suicidal move. At what he judged was the right moment, he plunged his sword upwards and was rewarded with the feeling of flesh parting against his blade. Without pausing, he shot down the length of the dragon, effectively slicing the entire belly open. Dropping his sword as he reached the bottom of the belly, Cormac continued his sprint. He would not die by being crushed by a massive corpse.

Cormac threw himself to the ground, rolling out from beneath the dragon, narrowly escaping death. The dragon's tail barely missed him as the creature thrashed in its death throes. The air was now almost sweet as it greeted the knight's lungs. He laid there, watching the dragon's last moments. In return, it gave one last feeble roar then collapsed onto the ground.

Adrenaline kept Cormac moving as he got up. He walked towards the head of the dragon and watched as the life faded from those great orbs. It blinked one last time and tilted its head slightly as if asking the knight, *why*. As Cormac looked on, he felt no triumph, only weariness. A great melancholy overtook him, and he wondered if a knight must always kill to defend. In the end, they were both playing out their roles in a story told a thousand times. Could the tale have ended any differently?

While he pondered, wisps of light began to dance across the now-still body. It was a wondrous sight, all the colours of the rainbow caressed the dragon as if mourning its passing. But as the body was illuminated, it began to change, shrinking and shrinking until it was no more than a man. Bits of golden armour hung off the body, and a river of red ran from his stomach. On the breastplate was a painted dragon.

The ephemeral tendrils reached out to Cormac, moving to surround the knight. "What? No…" Cormac tried to shake it off. He attempted to run, but his body would no longer obey him. Doubling over in pain, he cried out as he began to change. Scales sprouted, cutting through flesh. Nails grew long, his hands gnarled, and his bones began to shift. As his face elongated, the knight finally understood.

* * *

At first, Cormac lost his wits and succumbed to fits of mindless rage. In those periods, like those before him, he would attack villages. The one he tried to liberate from the last dragon's wrath was his first victim. With the curse, however, came some knowledge. In his dragon dreams, he learned that it was a faery's curse. Some knight, long ago, had cut down a sacred grove in his folly, and the curse had travelled from knight to knight ever since. Yet, like all else, the potency of the curse faded with time and bit by bit, Cormac regained his mind.

The now ex-knight thought himself a coward, for despite his predicament, he had no desire to die by the hands of another knight. Or, perhaps, that was his last heroic act, for he wanted no other to succumb to his fate. Whatever the reason, he hid himself and bided his time, hoping that the last of the curse would eventually fade as well. He dreamt of returning to the village, victorious. He dreamt of fame that led to a permanent position with a rich lord. He dreamt of the village elder's daughter as his wife and the children they would have.

But time passed him by without change while the world grew smaller. Each year, there were fewer and fewer places for a dragon to hide. When the Great Migration came and many of the Unseen abandoned their ancient places to make their homes in the Digital, so did Cormac.

At first, he rejoiced in the freedom to explore without fear of being discovered. He could embrace being a dragon without fear of passing on the curse. Oh, and he had such adventures. He visited a large data center, rows of servers maintained by hobs. He romped with other Unseen creatures in a revel, dancing to the beat of CPU cycles. But by and by, he fell back into despondency, missing his human life and mourning dreams unfulfilled. So, more and more he slept, giving himself to the fantasies that played behind closed eyes.

* * *

A whirling buzz woke Cormac out of his repose. The strange sound perked his curiosity, and he moved to rouse himself. Shaking off the cobwebs of memory, he swiveled his head this way and that to search for the origin of the noise. His nose flared as he caught a metallic scent, and he gave a little huff. He had not had any visitors since he made his home in this forgotten folder, and he certainly didn't welcome an uninvited one that had interrupted his reverie,

At first, he saw nothing, but he felt small legs crawl up his tail. He moved to get a better view and watched as a tiny four-legged robot inched its way slowly up his body. The robot was odd-looking, with a vacuum-like mouth. Tilting his head to one side inquisitively, Cormac reached with one claw and picked up the little thing, studying it. He had heard of such things in the Digital, tiny robots that humans made to perform certain tasks—scripts, they were called. Gently, he placed the robot back down on the floor. Much to his annoyance, it tried to climb back up his body.

With a small grumble, Cormac swiped at it. But instead of being knocked back, the little thing stuck to him. Blinking in surprise, the dragon shook his arm, trying to rid himself of it, but he had no luck. Cursing his lack of thumbs, he leaned down. Before he could try to pick it off with his teeth, he felt a prick.

He yelped more from surprise than pain. Dragonhide was tough, so he was surprised he had even felt it. Looking back down, he blinked once, then twice as he found that his claw was rapidly fading, and the effect was travelling up his forearm. There was still no pain, but he could feel the change all the same.

Cormac had no way of knowing that the script was a disk cleaning utility with an almost unholy attraction to wasted drive space. All he could sense was that he was dying. The magic slowly bled from him. He thought once more of the life he could have lived and of the life that was imposed on him. He thought knight thoughts, and he thought dragon thoughts. And he decided, after so long, that this was as good a way as any to end the curse.

MEMOIRS OF A FORGOTTEN KNIGHT

The dragon smiled and closed his eyes one last time. The wait was over.

The End

Renee uses her years of experience as a developer to write about the what-ifs of magic and technology. When she is not suspiciously peering at her computer for mischievous pixies in between her writing, she can be found roaming the streets with her family or gaming (whether it's video games, board games or table-top RPGs) with her similar-minded friends.
www.wiredcrow.com

Sometimes They Come Back
By Roland D. Yeomans

I am the Caretaker. The House is old, very old. Me? I cannot remember my beginnings. My end will certainly not be pleasant. But what is one to do?

The best one can with the tools at hand.

At least my days are not boring.

It was time. The sun smeared the sky with its bloody fingers as it sank into the grave of the black horizon. I walked the carpeted stairs to the attic. Now, to stir Her bed of Egyptian sands with my breath.

The roof above the attic tingled with the memories of spring rain and rustled with the echoes of soft snow falling from crisp December nights. Silent as the rise of mercury in a thermometer, I slipped into the welcoming darkness of the attic.

High from the left corner, words danced from the shadows, *"Has Horus fled from the battlefield so soon?"*

"Just about," I said, walking to the ever-rippling circle of living sand on my far right.

I could never make it out clearly. Just as well. When the time came that I could, I would never leave the attic. It had the novelty of making each entrance somewhat exciting.

"You are so brave," sighed the voice of spider-webs.

I shrugged. "What is brave? You need me. I come."

"You are right. That is not bravery alone. It is nobility as well."

I bowed slightly in Her direction as befitting the compliment. *Grande Dame* was not alive as one thinks of life. Nor was She eternally dead. She...subsisted. Or perhaps a better word might be *insisted*. Life, Death: they were but trifles to Her as She insisted on having Her way with each new-born day.

I bent and breathed over the circle of sand which smelled of cinnamon and sunshine tonight. The day must have been profitable for *Grande Dame* this time. But then, She was adaptable and far-ranging.

"How long have you been with us, Caretaker?"

"Since honor still had meaning," I smiled sadly and turned my back to leave before I caught a clear glimpse of Her descending to Her bed.

I stepped quietly down the stairs which now wore no shroud of black carpet. Glistening mahogany welcomed my boots as I made my way to the second floor. Time to open the shutters to let moonbeams feather the oval window whose glass was the spun dreams of children.

As I opened the shutters that were as black as the hinges of Hell, a broad hand fell upon my shoulder. A voice heavy as your worst sins growled, "Will She see me tomorrow do you think?"

"I think your life would be longer if She never sees you."

I turned. The Shadow had no body, only the black semblance of one. Once he had a body...before he doubted.

"Thomas," I sighed, "She is dreaming now. She might be that mote dancing in yonder moonbeam or the laugh in a little girl's eyes or the chess piece an old man is just about to move in the town below. When She calls, I will let you know...with sad heart, for you are my friend."

The Shadow stiffened. "My friend? Why?"

"Because you need one. We are both lost souls. Perhaps there is a strange magnetism that binds those who search but never find. Who knows? I only know that I am your friend."

"I need no friend," he gruffed and faded into the shadows cast by the flickering gas light at the winding hall's end.

A small, sad voice squeaked at my boots. I looked down. Mouse. Now, he was one who returned my friendship.

"A human who does not know he is naked will never seek clothes," Mouse said, looking up at me with eyes that were black pools of hard-bought wisdom.

Mouse owed his freedom to Napoleon's soldiers. The gust of bacterial air which breathed from the First Dynasty tomb they ransacked gave them the freedom of death. Other soldiers returned the favor by blasting the nose from the Sphinx. She took it badly...along with their lives.

Mouse rubbed his face with his tiny paws. "Not my fault humans are stupid greedy."

"No," I sighed. "We come by that naturally."

Was Mouse a ghost rodent or had the bacteria-infested air of the tomb changed him somehow? Another question I was not likely to get an answer to. Unanswerable questions wandered in herds inside my mind. And that, too, was another part of the human condition.

I bent, picked him up, tucked him in my safari-jacket pocket, and said, "Come, Mouse. We have rounds to make."

Sticking his white head above the pocket's rim, Mouse squeaked, "Do you think the Children will kill us tonight?"

I made a face. "I prefer not to be on the menu, thank you very much."

Mouse looked at me dubiously, and I said, "Besides, I caught a pedophile earlier today. You know how they like to play with them."

Mouse chirped, "Then, we might just live another

day. Though why we bother I do not know."

I patted his tiny head. "Always surprises await us, Mouse. Always."

I walked down the now crystal stairs, its faceted steps gems from the treasury of the Sidhe. Mouse's whiskers rustled like straw stems of an angry broom. I did not blame him. Doom breathed in the air, death whispered on the chill wind ,and no sure road to safety loomed ahead.

I looked about me. How to describe the great parlor of the House? Swim down the deep, black well of your imagination, and still you would not conjure the sights I now saw. The lush black curtains were warm-breath linen, fluttering from the breezes cast by long dead despairs. The cloths draped over tables shaped as forgotten sins were spider-silk, begging to be stroked. If you were foolish enough to do so, the cloths would be fed.

The walls flowed in red velvet currents of madness and desire. I ignored them. The paintings were a bit harder to ignore. They screamed, moaned, begged, their images changing constantly, trying to snare my weaknesses. I was safe. They were soulless and thus had no concept of the shape of love.

Once long ago, there were wild woods where now the House stood. In the center of those gnarled oaks towered one black tree, crooked and bold as the lies of Man. How many seasons passed over those woods none can say.

Then, abruptly in the space of a single night, the House stood where once the tall black tree loomed. A village eventually grew around it, the buildings born of the silently screaming oaks felled to make them. The village eventually went the way of all men, but greed called from the far blue mountains and the lush green coast beyond them. A hub for wayfarers was needed. A town slowly took shape over the ruins of the village, none asking what had killed that prior community. Foolish, blind men.

It was a long, tragic tale, the farce called Man. Before Pontius Pilate washed his palms or Babylon baked its first brick, Man was busy destroying himself with his need not to see dangerous truths warning him the path to his dreams led nowhere desirable. But I, of all men, was the last to point a finger.

Mouse brought me out of my brooding. "The Children come. Oh, Rameses have mercy! They come!"

Once the song of innocence sparkled in their eyes. Once their bodies were whole. Once they resembled something human. No longer.

Broken teeth filed, uncut nails long and sharp, souls no longer residing in their chests, they scampered all about me in the thankfully shadowy parlor. "Feed us. Feed us! Or we will feed on you! On you and your little mouse, too!"

I turned a sour eye to Mouse. "And here I thought they did not watch the DVDs I leave for them in the cellar."

The largest slithered to me. "The Magic Eye and the shiny biscuits it eats do not feed us! We need flesh. If not others, yours will do."

I forced a face of stone. Once I had been a warrior. What remained of him refused to let them see my fear.

"You have been roaming the halls for too long. In the cellar is one who preyed on children as once you were."

I smiled grimly. "He is fat."

"Fat!" they all squealed.

The largest skiddered a caricature of a laugh. "Fat! From his tallow, we will make many candles to light our way in the cellar. We are all but out of them. Come, brothers, sister! We feast. We feast!"

The female giggled, "Let us take our time with him! Take our time!"

SOMETIMES THEY COME BACK

The others took up her chant. "Take our time. Take our time. Take our time!"

Mouse looked up at me, cocking his small white head. "You have no shame over this?"

Remembering the dying, whimpering girl over whose body I had found the waste of breath now doing his own whimpering in the cellar, I said curtly, "No."

"You are a hard man."

I shrugged. "I am the Caretaker. I do what I must."

"You have made murderers of children."

"They were children long ago. No more. Murderers and the magic of this place have made them something *Other*. This way only the guilty suffer."

"You suffer from this. I see it in your eyes."

"Oh, I am guilty, little friend. Too guilty. Still, I endure what I must to spare others who may not so easily bear it."

"It is not easy for you," squeaked Mouse. "That is why I am your friend...and always shall be."

I tapped his head gently. "Come, the rounds are not yet done."

Mouse asked, "Have you searched all the cellar?"

I shivered, "Wotan, no! Its roots go all the way down to Chinese tomb-yards. I leave the exploring to the Children of the Night."

"And what of others there who find them in *their* exploring?"

"Then, they are searching where they have no right to be and so get what all such folk eventually receive."

"Which is?"

"More than they wanted or wished."

Mouse asked, "Why do you not leave?"

"I am needed here. For a long time, I was not. It is a hard thing not to be needed, especially for one such as I. Besides, I have been here so long now that the House would only follow me, spoiling the sleep and dreams of those among whom I traveled."

"Dreaming Rameses! You are a strange man, Caretaker," groaned Mouse.

My smile tasted of bitter memories. "You are just now realizing that?"

The Rounds. The term sounds like the House is capable of being traversed in a single night. But it is not. Its timbers could build a flying wall wide enough to block a bird migration; its many floors ever changing in number, its arches capable of spanning St. Peter's Square, and its occupants shifting constantly.

I just checked in on as many rooms and completed as many duties as I could fit into one night. Mouse helped with his constant chatter. I think he was glad for the company of someone almost normal in his existence. Me, too.

Most of the House was complete, *Grande Dame* tells me, when the first stars began to coalesce into Light that caressed the awakening planet. It could be. I was not there. I am old, just not that old. Besides, I think *Grande Dame* would consider lying to be shabby on her part. And while She is many terrible, dreadful things, shabby is not one of them.

A mad dog howled far away in the night, and Mouse groaned, "Not the Rougarou!"

I shrugged. "Better than Bast, wouldn't you say?"

"You mentioned my name?" purred a silky voice.

Mouse ducked his head back into my jacket pocket as I turned, smiling. "Well, there is a gargoyle on the roof. Why not a cat in the parlor?"

Bast's voice grew deadly. "Do not be so bold, Caretaker. You are no longer an Einherjar."

"*Once* means *Always* to an Einherjar, Bast. You know that. And even the Cat of Cats can walk into tangle-sap if she doesn't watch where she steps."

Bast, autumn-breathed, fiery-eyed. It was jarring to see a black house cat the size of a panther pad her way towards me, her muscles vibrating under her thick pelt. A keen, hungry intelligence burned in those glowing amber eyes. Particles of dust tumbled like brown snow from her furred lips as she purred. Dust? But then again, she was an old, old goddess.

"When are you going to let me eat that morsel in your pocket, Caretaker?"

"We fought once before over my friend. It did not end well for you."

"You were lucky."

"I was skilled. I still am."

"I have hunted and been hunted upon strange snows, Einherjar, yet still I live. What are you?"

"Loyal."

Bast laughed, "You are that, Caretaker. *Grande Dame* would be hard-pressed to find another valiant lost soul such as you."

Deathwatch beetles ticked anxiously behind the walls. They hungered after a journey of some three thousand years. I did not invite them. Let them eat one another. They should have waited for Victoria's locomotives to take them in style across the sands as had Bast.

Shipped for passage to America, not for her mummy, but for the precious linen wrappings tied tight around her body, Bast waited patiently among the other stolen mummies. At the time, pulp-hungry newspapers starved for anything linen upon which to print meaningless drivel for humans who did not read the pages but only lined their birds' cages with the priceless wrappings. Or so it would have been except for the bacterial spores embedded in those wrappings. Plagues not seen since Moses swept New England and bulged hospital wards and filled graveyards.

Strange creatures freed from their imprisonment still walked Massachusetts night-blanketed streets as townships found themselves mysteriously freed from their vagrant problem. Sadly, the number of missing children grew. But I was not the policeman of the world. I was the Caretaker.

Those long years ago, I did not mind Bast padding majestically through the front door as I opened it to water the Dryads as a favor to Artemis. The Greek goddess sometimes played chess with me during long winter nights. Ignoring me completely, Bast stalked fluidly to the fireplace, spun gracefully around thrice to curl up on the shimmering Golden Fleece upon the floor. The moment she did so, the long-dead logs burst into happy flames. She slept there some decades until Mouse sniffed at her, checking to see if she were alive or undead.

She was undead...and hungry. Luckily, Mouse was quick and my pocket near. Not so luckily, I had to remind Bast that all who lived in the House must abide by the House Rules. Chief of which was no one ate my friends.

Bast read my mind as she often did. "You should have let me eat him. One day, I will...after eating you."

I smiled my skull smile. "But not today. Want to help me water the Dryads in the twisted oaks?"

Bast sniffed the air tentatively. "Yes...and no. But I will greet the foolish mortals who are even now approaching the front door."

Her purrs as she strode beside me recalled the screams of the Hebrew slaves as they labored for the glory of the mortals foolishly thinking themselves immortal. The air began to smell of Egyptian sands and embalmed bodies. I willed a bit of oak, ash, and thorn to the mix for old times' sake. Amused, Bast looked at me out of the corner of her slit eyes.

Inside my pocket, Mouse quivered a plea, "Oh, please do not open the door to mortals. It always ends badly. Please do not."

I shrugged. "The sign on the front gate reads:

SOMETIMES THEY COME BACK

ENTER AT YOUR OWN RISK. If they are unwise enough to enter the grounds, their fates are their own doing not mine."

Bast laughed coldly. "Make your face stone as much as you wish. I am not fooled. I know your heart is warm. You hope to find *her* returned upon your doorstep."

"That was unkind," snapped Mouse, still wise enough to stay hidden in my pocket.

"I am Bast. What else did you expect of me?"

A wandering wind that came from nowhere and seemed to sigh everywhere breathed past us. The door was oak which pleased the Dryads and Artemis not at all. The House did not care. It did what it did. Most of the time, the House's actions made no sense to me even in retrospect.

There was a timid knock at the door. Then, a louder, bolder knock took its turn on the oak. I thought wearily to myself that none of us live the life we planned when young. Mouse squirmed inside my pocket, and to placate him, I spoke loud enough to make myself heard through the thick oak.

I made my voice a buttress against fools. "Go away. This is your only warning. Leave now and live your mundane lives. Enter and be damned. Both lives will seem long...but for different reasons."

Bast chuckled in the sound of breaking bones. "Do you really expect this warning to work?"

"No, but I tried my best."

"Your best," squeaked Mouse from my pocket, "would be to not to let them in at all no matter how long or loud they knock."

I reached into my pocket, tapping his head as if packing tobacco into an ancient, well-used pipe. "Have you forgotten about the howl of the Rougarou?"

"Oh, no!" cried Mouse.

"Yes, little friend. If they are not killed outright

but only infected, things will be worse. They are town-born. Wounded they will stagger to the town, heal, and then the first time they are angered, they will transform into werewolves. I am tired of facing maddened mobs of town-folks with pitchforks and torches."

The pounding took up again. Scowling in irritation, I waved a hand in front of the door: a gift from Freyja... for wounds endured for her sake. It disappeared as if it had been a candle's flame snuffed out between thumb and forefinger.

Twin yelps sounded from the sprawling expanse of the front porch. I took the two mortals in with one glance. Einherjar are taught to do so. Those who do not learn the art quickly learn nothing else since soon they are dead.

The pair were newsmen, though there was nothing new to the tripe they reported upon or about which they wrote. And only one of them was a man. The cameraman. Big; thick-bellied, smelling of lust and expectation. I sighed. It was plain he had plans for the woman later on in the evening whether or not she was willing.

The woman. For the first time in centuries, the still heart within my chest began to beat again. Peeking out of my pocket, Mouse groaned low.

She held a short stick that I believed was called a Mike, silly name for something. The woman wore a gossamer wisp of a green dress. Her blue eyes were wide-set, and there was thinking room between them. Her wavy hair was dull red like a fire under control... but still dangerous. A flood of memories swept me up. Mouse whimpered.

Bast cried out in delight, "Lustful mortal! Fair game. This one is mine. Mine!"

"Drake!" the woman reporter screamed.

It did no good. Bast was already upon him, her

bloody claws rending and slashing. A happy growl in her throat, she ripped at the yelling cameraman. The yells did not last long.

The woman beat at my chest. "Damn you! You set your panther on Dra..."

She stepped back. "All around your body...there's a strange golden light."

My awakened heart skipped a few beats. Only Valkyries could see the honey-gold auras around the bodies of the Einherjar. Mouse popped his head above my pocket and squeaked.

"Your name is Kára, is it not?" he squeaked.

The woman glared at me. "Throwing your voice is not going to keep me from getting the hell out of here and calling the police on you and your damn monster."

"What monster? And Drake who? There is no one and nothing beside you."

She spun about and hushed in a breath. "They're both gone!"

I said, "This Drake of yours..."

"Oh, god, he wasn't mine. He wanted to be bad enough though."

She shivered, and I said, "Yes, he did."

"How do you know?"

"He smelled of anticipation and lust. He was planning on assaulting you once you two were walking away from here."

The woman turned back to me, a familiar anger blazing in those blue eyes. I shivered. After so long, Kára was back. My Wild One was back!

Although like those other few, precious times, she did not remember me. Wotan, please let this time be different. Thunder rumbled above me. I sighed. Wotan did not like his warriors to beg. I reminded myself that I was no longer Einherjar.

I was the Caretaker.

HERO LOST: MYSTERIES OF DEATH AND LIFE

I forced my voice to be calm. "Be that as it may, the two of you were warned...twice. You ignored the warnings both times. The mayor, the chief constable, and I have an understanding: they give the House no problem, and the House does not drive them insane with nightmares. After a few weeks of *Grande Dame*'s nightly *gifts,* they agreed...agreed most enthusiastically."

"You blackmailed them!"

"The House did. And I prefer the term *'bartered.'*"

I waved towards the still open gate. "But be my guest. Report this incident to the constable. It will do you no good...except for saving your sanity. I was not lying...Miss. Enter here, and you will be damned. You may leave the House whenever you wish, but the House will never leave you. Please, go now!"

I shivered in the marrow of my bones as I felt *Grande Dame* reaching out past me to touch Kára's mind. I had a sinking feeling my spectral charge was wiping the memory of what happened to Drake from her mind. It would not happen all at once but slowly in stages until Kára acted as if she had come alone.

The azure eyes that haunted my dreams studied me so intently I expected my clothes to start smoldering. "There wasn't a lot of conviction in that last sentence."

"I...I have my reasons. Now, please leave."

Mouse leaned forward in my chest pocket. "He speaks truth. You must leave if you wish to stay safe...and sane."

She looked back to me. "You're good. It really seems like the little guy is talking to me."

She turned back to Mouse. "All right, I'll play along. Yes, mister mouse, my name is Kara. Kara..."

"Just Mouse," I interrupted. "And no last names, please. Last names are but hollow constructs. It is to our first names that we attach our essence."

Her eyes were skeptical. "Oh, really?"

"Really. During the late Middle Ages, a new class of men appeared...men of property and wealth, yet were not titled. They were proud, independent, and ingenious. They called such men franklins from the Middle English word, *frankeleyn*, meaning freeman."

I sighed, "When surnames became the vogue, families from the upper classes took on the name of their domains: Lancaster, Salisbury. Their serfs took on the name of where they lived: Hill, Meadow. Artisans took on the last name of their trade: Smith, Taylor, Weaver. But for free-thinking, ingenious, proud men, the only name that fit was Franklin. It fit Benjamin Franklin's nature, too. Sadly, it was a nature that also damned him in the end."

Kára studied me. "You are a strange man...which fits the tales told late nights in all the pubs about this house."

She turned playfully to Mouse as if this were some game and not a memory in the making that would later tear out my heart. "How did you guess my name was Kara, little guy?"

Mouse twitched his whiskers, whether in irritation at not being thought intelligent or whether in pleasure at the attention of another human, it was hard to say. He chirped his answer.

"You...remind me of a tragic Valkyrie. By accident her husband struck her down with his sword when she swept too low on her winged stallion as he fought hopeless odds."

Her hot sunset eyebrow arched. "You know many Valkyries, do you?"

Mouse's eyes welled with tears. "No. Only the one."

Kára looked troubled for a moment, but it quickly passed like a song that nibbles at your mind on the outer rim of memory. "Hey, I know the little guy's name. You know mine. But what is yours?"

I tried to keep my voice neutral, though I did not think I succeeded very well. "Helgi."

Kára's stormy eyes flinched slightly, but she said low, "You say it as if it should mean something."

"Only to me, Kára. Only to me."

Mouse nodded past Kára. "We were going to water the Dryads, remember, Caretaker?"

Kára frowned, "I thought your name was Helgi?"

I shook my head. "That was my name from...my other life. Here, I am called Caretaker."

"You are called by what you do?"

"There are worse things to be called, don't you agree? Besides, do we not become what we do? Come, let me introduce you to our Dryads."

I started towards the twisted oaks but paused. Their dryads were jealous of my attention. They might cause some of the gnarled branches of their charges to slash at Kára. Going against my nature, I decided to be prudent. I knew just the dryad to approach first. I followed the scent of cherry blossoms. I saw her almost immediately, caressed by the silken moonbeams. Starlight touched her as if through broken stained glass.

Cranea. Her otherworldly features were delicate, fragile ... just like her tender spirit and lithe body which nestled gracefully in a hollow of the cherry tree's trunk. When her tree died, Cranea would as well. I made sure to water and nourish it...and her... nightly.

Her face brightened when she saw me and literally glowed when she spotted Kára. "She is back!"

Kára had no time to ponder Cranea's words as the reporter gasped "She's naked!"

"Of course," bubbled the dryad in merriment. "Clothes would only tear when I sleep deep in the trunk of my lovely tree."

Kára cocked her head. "You truly believe you are

a dryad?"

Cranea smiled teasingly. "I believe you are right."

"But you do not leave this tree ever?" asked Kára.

"Oh, I do not need to. You see, my tree communes with Gaia Herself so I hear the language of the clouds and of the near seas and far. The gossip of the birds is mine whenever I am bored. There is so much in my heart and mind all the daylong that life for me, though short, is so rich!"

Kára frowned. "Short?"

Balanos, the dryad dwelling within the nearest oak, called out mournfully, "We of the Oaks are immortal. So to us, our dear sister, Cranea, will seem to flicker out like the passing of a firefly or the blossom of the moonflower whose bud lives but for the space of a full moon."

The Satyrs lurking in the bushes by the oaks cried out in sudden fear. There was a tumult of leathery wings, a collision of mists and anguished souls in ribboned smoke descending from the sea of distant stars, and the smell of never-ending hunger. Something out of Hell itself thundered to the grass.

The Jabberwock.

Eyes of flame, jaws that tore, claws that caught. I couldn't get a clear glimpse of its bulk only that it moved fast as beads of mercury across a tilted mirror. Its misshapen head cocked as if listening to some inner voice of secret sin. Its wilted lids covered empty eye sockets. A ghastly white vapor misted from its opening and closing jaws. The House had never produced the like before. Why now?

The icy whisper of shifting spider-webs spoke in my mind. *Grande Dame.*

'You created him, oh, my Caretaker. At least, you set the Cosmic Wheel into motion. This is the slayer of innocents you fed to the Children of the Night. They transformed him as a jest. Alas, the joke was upon

them, for he ate them. And now, he will eat your returned Kára if you are not the Einherjar that walked into my House so very long ago.'

Behind me, Kára swore in Norse, "Jeg driter i melka di!"

She looked startled. "What did I just say?"

Mouse furiously shook his tiny head. "Do not tell her!"

I snorted. I was not about to tell a soul-awakening Valkyrie that she had just told a monster she was about to defecate in his milk. And yes, it loses quite a bit in translation.

I swore a bit in old Norse myself. Once again, I had hurled myself back into my own midnights. The Jabberwock burbled in madness as it lumbered towards me in a speed nothing so huge should have been able to reach. It was more a scourge than ever he was in mortal form.

Now, he was a foul disease, an annihilation of crimson eyes, razored fangs, taloned claws, and the rasping snarl born of the screams from a thousand mutilated souls. The stoic calm of my centuries as Caretaker shed from me like molting snake scales. I was once again Einherjar.

I sneered at myself. Right then, a good sword would prove more useful than a Viking mind-set. Mouse squeaked in alarm as the saliva drooling from the Jabberwock's slavering jaws burned to a crisp the grass stems upon which they fell. I coiled to sell my life dear, buying time for Mouse and Kára to make their escape into the House.

I roared, "Brenn i helvete!"

But before I could rush the Jabberwock, two sharp explosions right beside my head deafened me. The Jabberwock's empty eye sockets spurted jets of black blood. He stiffened and then, toppled over like a puppet with the strings suddenly cut.

SOMETIMES THEY COME BACK

I turned quickly about. Kára, both arms outstretched, held a gun rock-steady as smoke trailed up from its barrel.

"You remember!" I cried out in joy, starting forward to wrap my arms around her.

She shook her head, her dark red hair becoming a living waterfall. "I *remembered* I always carry a gun in my purse. Especially going out on assignment alone. Damn that Drake. Why didn't he come along with me?"

Kára abruptly jerked the gun my way. "I get it that you think I am someone else re-born, mister. I do. That just makes you a dozen fries short of a Happy Meal and as crazy as the rest of this damn place. Don't come any closer. I mean it! Stay away."

Kára backed carefully away, the gun never leaving its aim at the center of my chest. When she was far enough away to feel safe, she turned around. I watched her sprint towards the open gate. As soon as she darted through it, Kára ran to her car, jumped in, started it, and floored the thing with the scream of protesting gears. Gravel sprayed the night as she raced away into the darkness and out of my life. Again.

Mouse gently touched my chin and said softly, "Sometimes they come back."

He cocked his head mournfully at me, the thickness of tears to his voice saying even he did not believe his next word. "Sometimes."

Far off near the Temple of the Moon, the desert winds whispered; between the paws of the great Sphinx, dust tornadoes danced; and somewhere in the darkness of the bordering woods, a wolf howled. My heart joined it.

The End?

HERO LOST: MYSTERIES OF DEATH AND LIFE

Roland Yeomans believes myths are secrets of the heart made manifest in prose. Then again, he has been wrong before. Born in Detroit, Michigan, now of Lake Charles, Louisiana, he has been a teacher, counselor, book store owner, but always a writer. You can find him at his blog, *Writing in the Crosshairs* - www.rolandyeomans.blogspot.com/ or on his Facebook Author's Page - www.facebook.com/Roland-Yeomans-AuthorKnight-Errant-1103005016429637/

The Wheat Witch
By Erika Beebe

Don't go home. That's what they'd said. His sisters, his mother, his father. But they hadn't killed a man.

He hadn't really been thinking when he'd backed out of that alley, blood on his fingers, on his shirt—God, was it even his?—and gotten in his car. But here he was, stale coffee in one hand, and his hip aching from the eighteen hour drive.

Dusty Kansas wind shoved the car and Ethan gripped the wheel. A car lazed against the fields further up the road. A cop? Sweat slid down his face. His gaze darted to the rearview mirror. Dim, gleaming light met his eyes. A car? The police? Had he been followed from D.C.? He took his foot off the accelerator. Then pressed down on it again. The engine growled at him. His stomach growled back. When had he last eaten? He glanced at his side mirror. Not a car. The sun. Dawn.

He swerved into the sleeper lane. The tires spun and squealed. Rocks clinked under the car. He cranked the wheel straight along the old dirt road and gritted his teeth.

A green sign rose up to greet him: Welcome to MannHigh. Across from it, a cemetery stonily judged him. He swallowed as he made the slow turn onto Main Street and rumbled over the railroad track. Home, he thought. He just had to get to his grandfather's farm. Then he could sort this all out.

A dog barked from a sagging front window and Ethan jerked from the noise, pressing down on the gas again. In his mind, he heard the sound of his fist hitting skin, again and again and again. He kept going; past the post office, a red brick building with a front window splintered with cracks and no sign.

Across the street, grain trucks lined around the corner of the co-op, ready to weigh their crops. A man in overalls stood next to a truck. He turned and waved at Ethan. Ethan pretended not to see him and gripped the stick shift so hard his knuckles turned white. If the town knew what he'd done...if they remembered him, he didn't want to think about what he'd have to do to stay free.

Don't let them see you.

He kept the speed limit through town and counted every red brick building along Main Street, more to keep his mind away from the brick building he'd left the body behind than because he thought he might get lost. The blacksmith shop, the grocery store, even the bank stood where he remembered. Those boarded windows hadn't been there when he'd left MannHigh at 16.

Further down the road, the old church and the high school buildings remained as markers on the edge of town—forgotten tombstones. Falling messes of brick, weeds and broken glass. The old baseball field had been mowed recently, but the bases and the bleachers were long gone. This is it?

Ethan almost missed the road to the farm. A post marked the mailbox but the head was missing. He reversed and crept down the long gravel drive. The sun spilled against the windmill, the grain tower, the barn, the shed; highlighting the rotted wood, the missing shingles, the gaping holes where a window once stood.

What happened?

He pulled his mustang up to the old shed and cranked down the window, ignoring the ache in his arm. The white two-story farmhouse still stood there,

THE WHEAT WITCH

but the roof was missing shingles and the paint had peeled off in places around the front window. His chest tightened. His breath came faster at the sight of his grandma's rocking chair ghostly still. A spindle of wood was missing from the center. The porch was broken too. The planks worn and flecked with pieces of paint. Strangely, the front door boasted glossy blue paint and a wreath of golden wheat hung high on the door. Someone had been here.

A gust of wind brought a sudden hint of fire, and a million memories popped into his head. Danger warnings, mostly, from his father, about flame and wheat and how quickly things could catch out here. If you didn't sense and stop a fire early enough, the whole town could burn down before the fire trucks from the next town received the message.

He pushed the car door open, shoved his keys in his pockets.

Down the hill on the side of the house, he swam through the weeds and crackly branches. Dust clouds hung in the air. His heels sunk in the dirt at the edge of the clearing. A patch of grass had been cut low and a burn pile stacked. Furniture, planks of wood, blankets, and old clothes blazed with fire.

Ethan's heart hammered. His stomach twisted with the smells. Rotting wood, burning metal, and something so foul he couldn't quite place it. He approached the fire and stood as close to it as his skin would stand. Flames ate an old couch and swallowed the fat curved arms, then moved up to a painting of sunflowers stacked on top.

Holy Christ. He covered his mouth. It was his mother's painting, the only thing of his mother's his grandmother ever hung in the house.

He had to get it. Sweat dripped down his face, but just as he reached towards the fire, a crack, loud as gunfire, sounded behind him.

Ethan threw his hands over his head as he spun, trying to see through the smoke. His heart slammed against his ribs.

"Hello? Anyone here?"

Flies buzzed around him. He swatted at them.

"Hello?"

Oddly quiet, Ethan walked to the tree line, the wilder part of the land. A pile of animal bones sat in the shadows. The rotted skin of a rabbit was nailed to the trunk of the tree. Strangely, no croaking frogs or chirping crickets. A branch snapped above him. He gazed up. A black crow flapped its wings and flew off. Goosebumps prickled his arm, but he kept walking. The old river bed cut through the property in a maze of lines. He stopped to wipe the sweat from his brow. His hands were shaking. This was not the land he remembered. Lush grass, water in the riverbed. Fields of wheat, soy and clover everywhere. Cows in the pasture and fences to keep them in. No, his grandfather's farm had been abandoned, the land had dried up with drought. He wondered if his father had known.

Ethan circled back to the clearing and stared through the trees at the fire.

There.

On the other side of the fire, a woman stood impossibly close to the flames. Even this far away, Ethan could see the determination on her face as the flames licked her hair.

"Don't!" Ethan scrambled around the fire towards her. He'd be too late. And then it wouldn't be just the smell of the wood burning.

The woman paused, turning halfway to face him. The glow of the fire cast her wrinkled features into shadow and orange light, making her seem both ghostly and familiar. An aunt...no. A cousin? Oh God.

"Please don't," Ethan said again. How long did it

THE WHEAT WITCH

take for someone to catch fire? Could he grab her back?

The woman's dress swirled in the flames. She was too close, too close. The fire climbed up her dress. She was going to...

She stepped away from the fire and Ethan froze.

The fire still burned at her, but she didn't seem to notice.

"I've been waiting for you."

"Please," Ethan said again. "You don't have to throw yourself in there."

The woman leaned her head back and cackled. Her eyes were the color of flame. "Just like you didn't have to run?"

Ethan's head spun. Was she a cop? She couldn't be. She was too old.

The old woman walked around him and the edge of her dress fluttered against his pant leg. He could smell the wheat all around her, grainy and fresh as a newly cut field. Her skin changed before his eyes. Her face, the wrinkles smoothed and her hair colored from gray to a strawberry blonde. Freckles dotted her rosy cheeks, like sparks.

Magic.

Ethan had been warned about wheat magic. He'd shared those warnings himself, back when that same magic had coursed through his blood and sang through the Kansas wind. Back when the farm prospered because of his family, because of him, because of the unnatural magic and strength the land had given them.

Ethan's pulse pounded in his ears as he tried to remember those cautionary tales. Politeness. Don't promise anything you can't keep or you'll sell your soul forever.

"Who are..." he started to say. His jaw hurt. He willed his mouth to move and finish his thought.

"How did you come by my grandfather's property?"

"Do you remember your first day of school?" The woman's voice surprised him, echoing through his ears, inside his head. He shook his head, and then blinked as pain ripped into his forehead.

"You were just a boy then, your hair yellow like the wheat. You said 'Morning ma'am. Ethan Isaac Klaussen.'"

Who? How? Why did you burn the farm? Questions he wanted to ask. His mouth wouldn't open. He couldn't make the words form. He tried to think. He had a feeling this woman wouldn't wait, but his head was killing him.

"Still nothing?" The woman circled Ethan. Her finger traced around his shoulder, his back, until she faced him again. Flame flickered in her eyes. "That morning, I said to you, 'Isaac is a fitting name. Then I asked if your faith in your family was strong like his.'"

He grabbed his head. The pounding was so intense he gagged. He forced the memories to the surface. The white school house. The front steps. A woman was standing there. "Say hello," his father had egged him on. He stared at her face in the sunshine. The light faded and suddenly Ethan remembered it all. His teacher.

"I told you I'd face my fate if it were God's will."

"That's a good start." The woman smiled and her gaze shifted to the field just over her shoulders.

"You can bring the life back. Your strength would return."

Ethan stared at the field. The weeds shimmered in the hot sunshine. They soaked in the light, and somehow the colors brightened from the brown of the dead weeds to shades of red and gold. Heads of wheat unfolded in the field just as thick and golden like he remembered of his grandfather's crops.

It wasn't possible.

THE WHEAT WITCH

Almost as soon as he thought it, the image disappeared, replaced by the burning inferno next to them.

"I won't give the answers away for free."

"Answers," Ethan said carefully. He remembered the stories, the ones about a witch that could pick the questions out of your head.

The woman picked up his wrist. She studied the lines on his palm. "You've done something you're ashamed of."

Ethan stiffened.

"Stay with me. Help me with the farm. Plant my fields. No harm will come to you here. You'll become a hero again."

Her voice shifted with other tones. He swore he heard his mother, then his sister Madalyn. Memories flickered in his head. Laughter in his grandmother's kitchen. The yellow wallpaper. His sisters kneading dough on the table. His father walking through the front door, burnt from the sun, smelling of harvest with a huge grin on his face.

"Ethan!" He heard his best friend, Abe, yell for him. Ethan said good-bye and ran outside, just a kid, and found Abe, bucked tooth and scrawny circling his grandfather's jacked up tractor. "Needs a tweak underneath. You're grandpa will thank me later," he'd said, the best damn mechanic even at 10. Skinny Abe crawled underneath, while Ethan shook his head and picked up the weed sprayer. Hot. July maybe. Ethan glanced back at the tractor. He watched it jerk when suddenly the farm jack collapsed and rolled to the side.

"Abe!" Ethan had dropped the sprayer and ran. A leg protruded, twisted all wrong. Abe screamed in pain...then silence. Blood soaked the grass. Faster than lightning, Ethan grabbed the tractor's front end and shoved it like paper across a desk or a rock he'd toss in the stream. Bloody and broken, Ethan carried Abe inside where his grandma used something to fix him. A finely ground powder that smelled like the fields.

"He's out cold. His bones will heal," she'd said when she finished.

Abe had healed. He'd become Ethan's pitcher then. And suddenly Ethan saw their high school, a baseball game in the field nearby while the entire town cheered from the bleachers. Up to bat, he'd missed the first pitch. His eyes had gone to the face instead of the ball. Not this time, and he swung. He sent the ball past the pitcher, the bases, and beyond the outfit. The crowd cheered his name. Afterwards, his dad had put his hand on his shoulder. "Ethan, no one can do what you do."

"That's what you want, isn't it?" The witch's voice brought him back. "That's why you ran here. You could've gone anywhere and yet, here you are. They could find you still, you know."

She was right. He knew she was.

Ethan exhaled the breath he'd been holding. He knew the legends, the stories. He could be trapped here forever. The witch could steal his life, his whole soul. He could go to sleep one day, like his mother, full of cancer no hospital could cure. He could wake up one day, like his sister, full of voices that weren't his, and be locked away in a place where people whispered things like mental illness and coping. But what other choice did he have? To keep running and hope the cops didn't catch him? Or accept this strange magic and stay in the place that he'd last known happiness?

At least if they caught him here, he could say he'd spent his last days somewhere good. He could pretend he was the hero again.

"I'll stay."

* * *

THE WHEAT WITCH

Ethan spent the first days cleaning—the house, the yard, the barn, the shed. The woman had returned only once since that first day to tell him there was a truck in the garage and that she'd be going to feed the chickens. He hadn't seen her since.

On the fourth day, he tore down a few rotted walls in the shed near his grandfather's old dressing room where his overalls once hung on the rusty hooks and gloves and boots sat on a raised board. The tiny sink was still there and caked with dirt. Ethan turned the faucet and dark water sputtered out. The wall above it was bare where once pictures had been tacked up. Black and white Polaroids of younger days with grandma, their first date, their first harvest together, and of course several of his four boys, Ethan's uncles. The shed seemed cold without them.

Ethan crawled on the tractor. He primed it, tried to start it, and it sputtered but wouldn't kick to life. Not now. He tried again and still got the same choking sound like it couldn't breathe in the shed either. He checked the headlights. Soft white beams hung in the shed. Bits of dust floated in the light, but they weren't bright enough. Had to be the alternator. He pulled out a rag from his back pocket and wiped the sweat from his brow. MannHigh was unavoidable at this point, but he'd never find the mechanic parts in the co-op. Another town meant more curious eyes. And how far did the witch's ring of magic go?

Ethan felt the burn of eyes on his back. A sudden breeze of air wrapped around him. He shivered with Goosebumps and turned around. "I still don't know your name."

The old woman's wrinkles lifted with her smile. "Ruby Warkentin. Use my account at the co-op to purchase anything you need. But mind your budget."

He glanced at the old ford truck across the dusty shed. "I'll take the truck and order the seed." He didn't

HERO LOST: MYSTERIES OF DEATH AND LIFE

really think it mattered where.

A sudden warmth tightened around Ethan's wrists, his ankles, shackle tight. Ruby smiled.

"Are you doing this?" He grabbed his wrist and winced from the squeeze of pain.

"It's a reminder. The pain will leave when the promise is fulfilled." Ruby turned and lifted a basket of grain to her hip. "I'm off to feed the chickens. You won't see me the rest of the day."

Ethan stood there and held his wrist. The pain lessened to something more tolerable. Had the witch done this to his grandfather too? He thought about their trips out of town. His grandfather had never gone to any of Ethan's baseball or basketball games outside the home high school.

Was it worth it?

He'd never know. His dad had hid his grandfather's illness and never gave him a chance to say good-bye.

Ethan crawled in the old farm truck. The springs bounced under him. He wrinkled his nose and he tried not to sneeze from all the dust. He primed the Diesel engine. It sputtered and sparked to life.

Back in MannHigh, he pulled into the co-op and walked in the front door. Smaller than he remembered, Elvis music played from a radio nearby. Shelves lined one wall with weed killer and gloves, hooks held smaller farming tools, hats and brand new boots sat on the floor underneath. On the other side of the room farmers sat at a table sipping coffee, swapping stories, and laughing.

"Howdy." One of the farmers nodded to him. "Welcome to town."

"Thank you," Ethan said low and approached the empty counter. A woman popped up from behind the register. He studied her closely. Just as closely as she studied him. Her light brown hair streaked with highlights rested over a shoulder in a ponytail. Her warm eyes sparkled and she smiled, her lips traced with a shimmery gloss. God, she smelled the same, of spring and flowers.

She covered her mouth with her hands. "Ethan Klaussen, after all these years. You're back."

"Hello Helena." He remembered the way she looked in high school, in her dresses her mom always made. Mostly yellows and light blues. She always looked so pretty, her hair nice, and she'd wait for him after his baseball games. That first kiss had been heaven. When he left, he swore he'd come back for her. Guilt hit him.

"Well, what can I do for you?" She leaned over the register.

"Fertilizer. I need lots of it. Weed killer. And wheat seed for sure."

"You want your daddy's usual?"

"How do you remember that?"

Her gaze shifted to the back wall. He followed her gaze. A painting, a precise map of the town, hung between a window and a shelf. Familiar bold swirls of color merged the sky with the wheat fields. Fat lines of color blended the homes and the town buildings into the landscape. Delicate strokes detailed people, faces, clothing, even hats.

"Your mother painted that. I think it was her first one. See how the town glows? Especially over your grandfather's property line?" She walked to it and stood on her tiptoes, pointing to the pastures and the windmill he'd remembered as a boy. He guessed the broad shouldered farmer on the John Deer was his grandfather. He had a special straw hat he wore and his mother had painted it in vivid detail.

"I forgot how much she loved to paint." Ethan cleared his throat and fisted his chest a couple of times. "Sorry. Allergies."

Helena handed him a box of Kleenex. "I figured

you'd get word somehow of your property up for sale. It sold though at auction back in the spring. Ms. Warkentin bought it. Did she get word to you?"

"Something like that. We've got an account..." He changed the subject.

"Yes. I know. The fertilizer is in the back. Get yourself a cart. You'll have to order the seed here and pick it up in Hilltown."

The next town over. Unavoidable, and unlucky.

Ethan turned to leave. He couldn't help but glance over his shoulder. "How did you get my mother's painting?"

"At auction. It wasn't me though. My brother Abe wanted it. He wanted all of them. Anyway, will you need equipment parts?"

Abe. His buddy. He was still around. Ethan didn't get it.

"Yes, for Ruby's old tractor. Where can I get those?"

Helena slid a loose strand of dark hair behind her ear. "Hilltown. The farm mechanic shop in the center of town has everything you need."

Ethan's palms were sweating. He adjusted the collar on his neck. "Thank you," he said and walked outside. He loaded his bags of fertilizer in the bed of the old truck.

* * *

Days past. A week. Ethan had done all he could to patch the roof on the house, cover the holes in the shed with sheets of metal the witch had left, and test and tweak the farm equipment. He needed to get the tractor running. He'd have to plow the field soon.

Inside the shed, night crept in. Ethan could barely see. His footsteps echoed against the cement floor as he walked. He found his flashlight and left the shed, studying the shadows, the sliver of moon above him. The hairs on his arms lifted. The feel of eyes on his

THE WHEAT WITCH

back made him shiver.

Where was Ruby?

He tried not to slam the front door. The house smelled of bleach. The wallpaper had been stripped off all the walls.

"Hello? Ruby? You here?"

No answer. He knew she wouldn't be. In the weeks he'd been on the farm, he'd studied her, too. By day, he'd see glimpses of her feeding the chickens or carting away more trash to the burn pile. By night, she'd vanish. No trace of her in her bed or the house. The tales he'd always heard growing up, warnings mostly, to never wander out in a field by night still haunted him, and probably always would.

Exhausted, Ethan showered and scrubbed the dirt from his body then fell asleep to the sound of the wind rattling the west window in the bedroom.

* * *

The next day, Ethan gassed up the old farm truck and drove to Hilltown. The tractor's alternator sat in the seat wrapped in a towel. Ethan passed an ALCO, a Phillip's gas station, and a line of specialty shops and restaurants. Down a side street, the glare of the sun highlighted a white car. Lights on the hood. A cop. Ethan hit the gas too hard and jolted forward against the wheel. Just his luck. He sat up straighter and kept going down the road, checking the side view mirror. The cop turned the corner.

Ethan saw the repair shop sign and turned carefully into the drive. He wiped his sweaty hands on his jeans. Lights flashed behind him.

He was done.

A car door slammed. The sheriff knocked on his window. Ethan's hand shook as he rolled it down.

"Morning." The sheriff gave him a once over. "License please."

Ethan handed it to him.

The sheriff looked Ethan over, then back to the license. "You're the last Klaussen. Come back to claim your land?"

"Hoping to someday. Right now, I'm just helping out Ms. Warkentin." Ethan lied.

"Don't know why she bought your grandpa's place. Not sure if I can remember the last time I saw a good crop out there."

The sweat dripped into Ethan's eyes. "So what did I do?"

"Taillight is out. Your D.C. license is two days from expiration. Get it taken care of. Or you'll see me again, from behind bars."

He handed the license back to Ethan and walked away. Ethan leaned his head back against the seat and forced several slow breaths through his paralyzed lungs. Then he grabbed the alternator and walked into the open garage door. A taillight. He smiled. Thank god that was all.

Ethan walked around the building, past the parked tractors in the lot out front. Inside the garage, a T.V. played from somewhere in the back. The cement floor was new. A couple of lifts held tractors and an old Ford truck off the floor.

"Hello?" he called.

"One sec," Ethan heard.

Something rolled across the floor, footsteps echoed, then a tall man with thinning hair approached. Grease streaked his work shirt. His smile gave Abe away.

"You're a sight for sore eyes, Ethan Klaussen."

Ethan shook his old buddy's extended hand. "Nice to see you too, Abe. Still got the same awesome strength in your hands."

Abe let go of Ethan's hand at once. "As I recall, you're the one with the strength. We were something back then, weren't we?"

Ethan smiled then held up the towel. "Think you

THE WHEAT WITCH

can fix this?"

Abe took the alternator. "You cleaned it up pretty good. I can run some tests. If I can't resurrect it, I'll swap you a new one at no cost. I owe you."

Ethan froze, thinking.

"We're even. Isn't that what you told me once?" Abe's words jarred Ethan's memory. Christmas. The last one at the farm. Ethan gave Abe his own gift, a brand new baseball glove. Hadn't mattered if it was perfect. His friend didn't have one anymore.

"Helena's not the only one glad to see you back."

He pictured Helena. Her beautiful gray eyes. Her smile. She'd hadn't been wearing a ring on her finger. Maybe...no. His past was too scarred to bring anyone else into his life, and all he'd ever trusted was his Mustang.

Ethan shoved his hands in his pockets. "I don't like your deal."

"It's done. How's your sisters?"

"Maddie's not good. Don't hear from Jos at all."

"I'm sorry. Let's go to the front of the shop and square up. Besides. I've got something of your mother's to show you."

Ethan stood to attention.

At the front of the shop, a couple of soft couches sat against a wall near a table and a register on the counter. Sure enough, a painting hung on the east wall of the shop above the register.

"No matter how you stare at it, the lines make you see something different every time. There's a woman in there, in all those swirls." Abe traced a circle in the air in the center of the painting. "My dad always said the woman there is the reason your grandpa's farm did so well. He called her the wheat witch. By saving her life in that blizzard...see swirl of the storm in all the hidden blue lines of the winter wheat?"

Ethan did. It was like a painting within a painting.

HERO LOST: MYSTERIES OF DEATH AND LIFE

The outer layer was summer and happy days. The inner layer was winter, of a storm and the dangers of life back then in the cold.

"My dad said the witch bespelled your grandfather's land as payment for her life."

Ethan rubbed his wrists. If Abe had known the half of the story. The way she'd bound their lives to the land, Abe would grow a brain and move away. Ethan would have.

The register dinged. "There. All taken care of. Need anything else? I mean...I'd be happy to make a visit to the place and check out the rest of the farm equipment. I could..."

"No. You've done enough."

"Really...I'd love to see all the old 60's auction pieces Ms. Warkentin bought. It would be..."

"Abe. Thank you, but no."

Ethan's back steamed, sweat threatened to stain through his shirt. This was not the time for Abe's persistence. What if he found out about Ethan's past?

"Ok. I get it. I'm backing off." Abe held his hands up in surrender.

Ethan didn't believe him, but forced a smile. "Thank you."

Ethan drove back to the farm thinking of the painting. He'd memorized the swirls, every shade of blue in the center, of winter, of the old man lifting the woman up with one hand and holding the reigns of his horse with the other. After living with the witch and the magic, he knew the painting had been a real event, but how had his mother known?

Back at the farm, Ethan spent the next week repairing the roof on the shed and ripping up the front porch on the house. It felt good when he replaced every last joist and sat his grandmother's repaired rocker on the newly stained planks. "This would make you proud," he said out loud to the wind and as if in

THE WHEAT WITCH

answer, the chair rocked. His cheek warmed as if he'd felt her soft kiss.

Wind gusted across the front yard. Ethan held his hat on his head. "I didn't ask you to fix the porch," Ethan heard the witch say from behind him.

Steady. His heart raced as he turned to face her. "My grandma wouldn't have forgiven me if I'd left it like it was."

The witch smiled, the fall breeze lifted strands of hair around her shoulders. She walked away and Ethan crawled into the truck and went back to Hilltown. He'd actually made Ruby smile.

Inside the co-op in Hilltown, Ethan asked about his order. The guy at the register seemed friendly enough and disappeared in a room at the back. Ethan walked around, whistling to himself, fingering a few grooming items on a shelf near the wall. He could use a good haircut. Maybe a new toothbrush. When he turned around, he dropped his things. Another painting of his mother's hung high above him. It was the largest one yet, another painting within a painting. Day on the outside; night swirled within the layers of a field on the inside. He studied it, sweating, the blood pushing hot through his veins. There, in the center, was a whisper of a woman, an angel, hovering over the wheat.

Ruby.

"Your order's ready. Go on around back and load it up."

Ethan felt sick. His mother had foreseen the fallen town. She'd painted it with exact detail to the rubble of brick.

There. He found his mother's name on a tombstone in the cemetery. She'd painted her own grave, alone, with no family stones around it.

Ethan ran for the restroom and threw up his guts. His heart pounded with his head. Her last moments came back. The nights in the hospital. The screams of terror, his mother's bruised circles under her eyes and all over her arms.

"I'm sorry I failed you and your sisters. I was an outsider Ethan, and the land, the magic, was too much. We left too late. I love you." His mother's last words. Back then he'd shrugged them off. He'd kissed her cheek and she'd passed.

Ethan washed his face, loaded the seed, and picked up the alternator from Abe at his shop. He swore then to himself he'd finish his promise, and sped back to the farm, eyes blurry with tears.

We left too late. He kept thinking about his mother. Had the witch killed her? He had to know.

Night swallowed the land. Ethan parked and jumped out of the truck. Standing at the tree line, fireflies blinked in the field.

"Did you kill my mother?" he screamed to the night.

* * *

Over the course of the next week, Ethan found it hard to eat. He plowed and planted like he'd promised, all the while, searching for the witch. He'd see flashes of her, heard the clucking of chickens, but when he thought he finally heard her voice or saw her outline in the trees, he'd arrive and find shadows and sunshine.

Exhausted, he fell on the edge of the field and gazed at the sunset. The field was done. Plow lines ran parallel in the dirt where the seed had been planted. The fall air rustled the leaves above him. The hairs on his neck rose. He turned around and met Ruby's gaze.

"I tried to save your mother. The cancer went too fast and too deep. Your father made his choice. I'm sorry."

Ethan's eyes burned with tears. He wiped his face

with his sleeve. "Her heart was stronger than all of ours put together."

A faint rumble of thunder startled him. Something wet splattered across his cheeks. Ethan looked up to the dark sky. Clouds built up like mountains and flickered with lightning. He didn't understand. Rain hit the dry earth with a soft thump. Then the whole field suddenly pattered with it.

"I release you from your bond."

The shackles around Ethan's wrists released. The blood rushed faster under his skin to his fingers.

"Stay if you choose. Be my heir. Or return home and face your fate."

Ethan stared at Ruby. Dry and unruffled, the rain and the wind hadn't touched her. But as she walked to the field, light outlined her figure. Her human form faded as she walked the rows of planted seed, her outline a million blinking fireflies. Thunder cracked. The fireflies scattered and danced over the field and in the rain.

Ethan jumped. His car keys suddenly stabbed him in the leg from his pocket. He dug them out and walked into the shed where his perfect red '69 mustang sat.

He opened the door and caught a flash of his face in the rearview mirror. No dark circles under his eyes. He made his choice and started the car.

* * *

Back in D.C. three days later, after a shower and a shave, Ethan waited at the bus stop. The police station was too far to walk. He stared at his hands. Stronger somehow, he felt healthier than he had in years. His knees hadn't hurt him when he woke. His knuckles and wrists weren't swollen with arthritis. Would it stay? He didn't know and it didn't matter anymore.

The smell of diesel filled the air. The bus growled

as it pulled down the street. Cars zoomed by. People passed in their black coats and black shoes. Everyone looked the same here. Ethan sighed. He missed the farm.

The bus door swung open. Ethan looked up and dropped his coffee. It couldn't be. A ghost? He stared at Chase, the man he'd killed.

"Ethan?" Chase jumped off the bus steps and hustled straight at him. "I've been looking everywhere for you. You weren't at work. Of course you couldn't have been, they'd told me you'd retired and were off on some vacation."

Ethan backed himself against a wall. "You're alive?"

"Buddy! On or off?" The bus driver yelled from the door.

"Wow. Must have been some vacation. Yeah I'm alive. Thankfully. Don't get me wrong, you knocked me out good. I was even pissed for a good couple of months. But you know what? My head got better and I hadn't had that much time off in awhile. My wife and I, well, we actually got to know each other again and liked it." He looked back over his shoulder. "He'll be there. Hang on!"

Ethan coughed. "I thought I killed you."

"Hell no! You kidding?" He beat his chest. "Better than ever. But I'm off to meet the wife. You saved us both. See you man."

"Yeah," Ethan said, stunned. "See you around."

Ethan got on the bus. The bus driver scowled but took Ethan's change and Ethan walked to the back of the bus.

"This one's empty." A familiar voice said on his right.

"Helena." She was here. More beautiful than ever.

"I've never seen the capital before. I've never left home. It's time I did."

THE WHEAT WITCH

Ethan sat down next to her. He took her warm hand.

"I've got all day to show you the sights."

The End

Inspired by her first grade teacher's belief in her imagination from the first story she ever wrote, Erika has been a storyteller ever since. A dreamer and an experiencer, she envisions the possibilities in life and writes to bring hope when sometimes the moment doesn't always feel that way.

Working in the field of public relations and communications for more than fifteen years, she has always been involved with writing, editing, and engaging others in public speaking. Her first short story "Stage Fright" was published in the young adult anthology, *One More Day* (J.Taylor Publishing, 2013).

Her two young children help keep her creativity alive and the feeling of play in the forefront of her mind

Facebook - www.facebook.com/ErikaBeebeAuthor/

Twitter - Erika Beebe@cloudninegirl1

Blog - Cloud Nine Girl www.erikabeebe.com/

The Last Dragon
by Sarah Foster

The orange light of the setting sun shimmered on the skeleton of the dragon. Every inch of bone—from the rows of sharp teeth in its mouth down to the tip of its tail—had been dipped in bronze after they boiled its flesh away. It stood in the exact place where it had been killed, in the middle of a lonely field with dry, brown grass. Even though its mouth had been propped open to make it look alive, as if it could burn you as you stood before it, it wasn't as frightening as I'd imagined. A dragon isn't so scary without its fire.

"I thought its teeth would be sharper," I said, staring at the dull bronzed points.

"It doesn't seem real, does it?" my sister asked, coming to stand beside me. Neither of us ever saw a dragon when they lived. We'd heard stories, seen drawings, but only this statue remained.

"This thing could only kill you if it fell on you."

Irillya laughed but only once. "It's getting dark. We should make camp."

I gazed up at the dragon. I'd thought they were bigger. If it had been alive, spreading its massive wings, perhaps it would have been. "How long until we get there?"

"A day. We should leave once the sun comes up."

I turned from the dragon and walked over to my sister. "Do you think he moved out here to be close to that thing?" I asked, pointing back to the bronze skeleton.

"No," she said, not even looking at it.

We built a fire and ate enough to keep our

stomachs calm. The journey had been long, and we didn't want to weigh ourselves down with too much, but our food grew low. Illy said it didn't matter. We just needed enough to get there. The rest would sort itself out. She was sure, and I couldn't question her.

Perhaps the strangest part of this journey was just being out in the world. The further we went, the less people we encountered, but still, it was quite the change. Three days into our journey, we saw a river for the first time. We'd come across trees so tall we couldn't see the tops and animals we never knew existed. We felt free, but we also realized the truth about the way we lived.

We'd been hiding most our lives, for one very specific reason. Our mother hoped to live in the world, to pass us off as merely brother and sister. But there was no denying it. We had silvery-blond hair, icy-blue eyes, and the same bone structure. Anyone who looked at us would instantly know we were twins. It was too dangerous to risk.

We lived in a quiet village where people didn't ask questions, and no one was greedy or brave enough to sell us out to the Black Cloaks. Mother fell ill quite often from the stress, which got worse when Illy turned twelve and began to show signs she was Gifted. Mother didn't even want us to leave the house anymore. She knew it wouldn't be long before my Gift began to show, and if people found out, we'd be in even greater danger. But five years passed, and I still showed no sign.

Illy was a Seer—a rare gift. She could have a vision at any moment, showing her some moment from the future that would come to pass. We'd heard of Seers, but no one actually knew any. And me, well, I was just normal. It was quite strange. A Gifted person with a normal twin—it was simply unheard of. Twins were always linked by magic. That's why the Black Cloaks wanted them. But a seventeen-year-old without a single sign of a Gift, that was even less likely. Every day, I was more convinced of what I had always known—I wasn't the special one.

Illy still believed my Gift would emerge. I'd ask if she saw this in a vision, but she said no. She had no proof, but that didn't matter. She said it was my own fault, that I was afraid of being Gifted. I didn't want it, so it didn't want me. She knew me too well.

Being Gifted used to be a blessing; it gave you a purpose in life. Back when there were dragons roaming the earth, someone like Illy could have seen one coming and evacuate an entire village before it was destroyed. Others were strong enough to fight, some controlled minds and even the dragons. One by one the dragons fell, until the last one. Its death brought peace, but it was short lived. A new evil took the dragons' place.

They were called the Black Cloaks because of the hooded capes they wore. No one knew if they had a real name. No one really wanted to know. Now there were no monsters to fear anymore, only men. Monsters kill simply because it is in their nature. Men do it for a reason.

They saw the Gifted as a commodity, something to use. Something to collect. No one knew how many Gifted had disappeared over the years. Everyone lived in fear. The Black Cloaks took whatever they wanted by forcing Gifted prisoners to use their powers. They controlled the whole kingdom. Rumors said they had a Mind Bender controlling the King, but they'd never admit it. It was over. The Black Cloaks had won. But they still collected the Gifted.

We watched the fire as the light of the sun disappeared. We needed to sleep. Only one day remained in our journey, and then our next one would begin. I opened my mouth to say this, but then I saw

THE LAST DRAGON

Illy's eyes. They went wide, as if she'd seen something horrible. Sometimes she did, but I wouldn't know until her vision ended. I moved around the fire and sat in front of her. Her head tilted back, and her eyes turned white. Each vision was different, but they never lasted long. When her mouth fell open, and her eyes shut, I knew the end was close. I grabbed her shoulders to center her back to the earth.

"What was it?" I asked, shaking her gently. "Was it Mother? The Black Cloaks? Did you see Uncle?"

She blinked a few times, and the blue of her eyes looked back at me. "I saw...fire."

I released her and sat back. "Fire? That's all?"

She shook her head, placing her palm to her forehead. "I don't...it wasn't clear." She huffed, stood up, and began pacing around the fire. "I *hate* visions like that. Useless."

Some visions weren't always clear, and those frustrated her the most. In the old days, we could have found another Seer—an experienced one to train her, but the Gifted kept to themselves now. If another Seer was out there, he was either in hiding, or worse.

She kicked at the ground. "Stupid...*fire*."

I chuckled. "Well, there is a fire in front of us."

She glared at me. "This isn't funny, Raynor!"

"Maybe it was a dragon."

She shook her head.

I glanced over my shoulder. The light from the fire bounced off the bronze skeleton. "There are no more dragons," I said, looking back at my sister. "Uncle killed the last one, remember?"

"It wasn't a dragon! It was just fire."

Illy was happy to put out our fire and go to sleep, although I knew her vision would keep her up for quite some time. What did it mean? There was no way of knowing when this vision would come to pass, but we had to trust them. One of her visions started us on this journey to find Uncle, but that one had been much clearer. That's what scared me.

I couldn't sleep, either, but I wasn't thinking about fire. I was thinking about that dragon. I couldn't see it in the dark, but I felt it. Really, I was thinking about Uncle, even though we'd never met him. Tomorrow that would change.

We'd heard the stories—other children telling the tale of the last dragon and the hero who saved us all. Illy and I would always exchange a secret glance, knowing we couldn't tell anyone the hero of all those stories was our mother's brother. Every story ended the same—not long after the dragon fell, the hero disappeared. No one knew what happened to him, and neither did we. If Mother knew, she didn't tell us, no matter how much we begged.

I knew our mission was part of something bigger, but I had to admit it excited me to learn how those stories ended. Why did he disappear all those years ago? Why did he stop being the hero?

We rose with the sun the next morning, eager to continue. As we left the barren field, I kept glancing over my shoulder to catch just one last look at the dragon. I'd wanted to see that statue my whole life, and now we were leaving it behind.

"What if he says no?" I asked as we walked what I hoped would be our final steps.

"He can't. He won't." She was always so sure, so confident. I envied it at times. I could never be as bold or brave as my sister. But when you can see the future, you can be sure of anything.

The sun burned high in the sky when we finally saw a billow of smoke rising in the distance. Illy stopped and grabbed my arm. Her fingers were tense around me. We followed the smoke and heard noises as we approached. First a strange cracking noise, and then a loud grunt. We glanced nervously at each

THE LAST DRAGON

other but continued. We were deep in the forest now, away from any roads or fields. Uncle didn't want to be found. What would he say when he saw us?

A small clearing came into view, just big enough for a tiny, stone house with a garden beside it. Smoke rose from the roof. A man chopped wood in front of the house. He was tall, with broad shoulders, long brown hair, and a short beard. He lifted the axe above his head and brought it down, grunting as it sliced through a thick piece of wood.

"That's him," Illy said as we hid behind the trees.

"Are you sure?" For some reason, he wasn't what I had pictured. He looked strong, yes, but worn. Tired.

"Positive."

"He doesn't look like a hero."

"Have you ever seen one?" I didn't know what to say to that.

"Who's there?" Uncle shouted, resting the back of the axe on his shoulder. "I don't like visitors and neither does my axe."

Illy took a step forward, but I grabbed her arm and shook my head.

"Come on, now," he said. "Or do I have to go chopping through the trees to find you?"

"No, wait!" Illy shouted, dragging me with her as we emerged from the trees.

Uncle took the axe in both hands, ready to defend himself as he stepped forward. Then he stopped, looked us up and down, and lowered his axe. "Oh, bloody hell," he muttered.

Illy stood up straight; her confidence boosted by the fact that he wasn't trying to kill us anymore. "Sir Mikah, we're..."

"Do you think I wouldn't know my sister's children?" He threw the axe down and turned toward the house. "Come inside. I'll make some tea."

Illy and I looked at each other. Our mouths fell

open. How did he know who we were? I shrugged and followed him to the door. Illy wasn't too far behind. What else could we do? We were there to see him, after all.

The inside of the house seemed even smaller. There was a bed, a table with a few chairs, some shelves, and a fireplace with a tiny fire crackling softly inside. Mikah set a pot of water over the flame to make the tea, but he didn't say anything to us. This all felt strange. It didn't feel like we were meeting a long-lost relative, and it certainly didn't feel like we were meeting a hero.

We sat at the small, wooden table with our teacups, and no one said anything. Mikah cleared his throat and looked up between the two of us with a forced smile. "So, here you are, then. Raynor and Illy."

"How do you know what they call me?" my sister asked. We assumed he didn't know anything about us.

He pointed at me. "Your brother came up with it. Couldn't say Irillya. Hell, I can barely say it."

"So, you knew us?"

"Knew you? I lived with you until you were about three. Your mother never told you?"

We shook our heads. "There's a lot she never told us," I said. "I'm surprised we knew you existed at all."

"Well," Illy said, "we had to. All those stories. The great Dragon Slayer. We bothered Mother with it so much that she finally told us the truth."

"Did she now?" Mikah asked, looking at his tea as if he wished it would turn into wine.

"She didn't tell us why you left," I said. "No one seems to know that."

"Good. Your mother was always smart."

Illy and I kept glancing at each other, hoping the other would figure out what to say. I wondered when she was going to tell him the truth, why we were really there. And I wondered why he hadn't asked.

We made small talk for a while. Mikah wanted to know how our mother was doing, how our lives had been. He didn't offer any information about himself, though. We were desperate for it, for those answers we'd wanted all those years—the ones that were even more important now.

"Do you know what's happened to the kingdom?" Illy finally asked.

He shrugged. "Aye, I know. It's part of why I left. I don't want anything to do with those damn Black Cloaks."

"But...you were a hero. You killed the last dragon. Surely you would want to stop..."

"Things change."

A long, uncomfortable silence followed, broken only by the occasional sipping of tea. How could this be the hero we wanted? Illy stared at her cup as she clutched it nervously between her hands. "There's something they never say in the stories," she said.

"What's that?" Mikah asked, not even lifting his eyes from his tea.

"If you're Gifted."

He made no expression, only tilted his cup back and drank the last of the tea inside. When he looked back, Illy's eyes were wide with wonder. "Well?" she asked. "Are you?"

He frowned. "Listen here, I sure as hell didn't need any Gift to kill that dragon. I just needed my sword. And luck."

"But you *do* have a Gift?" I asked. He had to, of course. He could have just said no.

"That's my business, and I've spent my whole life keeping it that way. I'm not about to tell my secrets just because you two show up on my doorstep with your children's stories."

"That's not why we're here," Illy insisted.

"Oh?" he said, raising an eyebrow.

"We came for your help."

"Well, you came to the wrong place. I don't help people anymore."

Illy looked at me, expecting me to say something.

I shrugged. I didn't know what to say.

She looked back at Mikah. "You don't have a choice."

"Is that so?"

"Look, you may not be Gifted, but I am. I'm a Seer, and I've seen the future. Your future. I've seen a great battle. I've seen you fighting the Black Cloaks."

He looked at her. Disappointment flashed over his eyes before his face turned to stone. He stood up. "You're wrong. You've got the wrong man."

Illy stood up quickly, slamming her hands on the table. "I'm *never* wrong. If I've seen it, it will happen."

"What exactly would you have me do? Take them all on by myself?"

"You'll have us."

"Two children. Yes, you have a Gift, but what good is a vision in a battle?"

"Maybe if you told us about your Gift…"

"To hell with Gifts! What good has a Gift ever been to anyone? All it does is get you snatched up by the Black Cloaks. Why do you think you've been in hiding your whole life?"

"You're just scared."

"You're damn right I'm scared. And you should be, too. You should have stayed home, little girl." He ran his hand through his long hair. His mouth was tight with anger, and then he pointed at us. "You can stay here tonight, but in the morning I want you gone." He went outside and slammed the door.

Illy and I looked at each other, but neither of us knew what to say.

We slept on the floor. It was nice to sleep inside,

except for the fact that I couldn't sleep. What were supposed to do if Mikah didn't come with us? Illy had always been so sure of her vision. He would come, and he would fight. How could she be wrong?

I wasn't sure what frightened me more—the vision being wrong, or if it came true. Part of me felt relieved at the thought of it never coming to pass. Mikah was a huge part of it, but another part had always been clear to Illy. Me. I stood beside Uncle as the Black Cloaks approached. It seemed so wrong, so improbable. I couldn't fight, I had no Gift. I had no place there. It terrified me more than anything.

In the morning, Mikah gave us breakfast, but he didn't speak. I watched Illy the whole time, the way her eyes moved back and forth as she tried to think of what to do. But what could we say to convince him?

When he was ready to shove us out the door, Illy turned to him. "Uncle, please. I know if you come with us, we can fight them."

"You don't know anything," he said, holding the door open.

Illy stood her ground. "If you would just tell us..."

"Damn you!" He slammed the door. "You want to hear a story? I'll tell you one. Sit."

Illy and I exchanged a nervous glance, but we sat down at the table. Mikah stood in front of us. "We have something in common, you know. A dead father. Your father never even knew there were two of you. He died not long after your mother found out she was pregnant. Months later, she was carrying too heavy, so we went to a Healer. And she told us. Two babies. Your mother was terrified. The Black Cloaks were known to rip twins from their mother's arms as soon as they were born. Gifted or not, it didn't matter. The potential for power was too great to pass up. I had to hide her."

Illy folded her hands. "Why did you leave?"

"Three years I stayed with my sister and helped take care of you. We were happy. Then we were found."

"By the Cloaks?"

"Not exactly. By my father."

"What do you mean?"

He sighed and shook his head. "My father was the first leader of the Black Cloaks. He created them."

"You can't be serious," I said. His father—our grandfather—was the one who started this madness? Mother never said, never even implied. How could it be?

"Do you think I would make this up? People saw me as a hero, a great warrior, the slayer of the last dragon. And my father was the evilest man to walk the earth. My own blood was my greatest shame."

"What happened?" I asked.

"He saw you, both of you, and he nearly went mad. 'Two of them,' he said, his eyes wide like a poor man who'd stumbled upon a chest of gold. I tried to plead with him. 'They're your grandchildren, not pawns in your war.' It made no difference. He would have taken you. So, I did what I had to."

He stopped and closed his eyes as if he didn't want to go any further.

Illy cleared her throat softly. "What you had to?"

"I killed him," he said, slamming his fist against the table. "I killed my own father. I never once hesitated when I killed that dragon, and I didn't hesitate then, either. I knew what had to be done. But I wasn't going to pat myself on the back or make some bloody statue. I still killed my father. It wasn't easy. I found a new place for your mother and then I left."

"So we could be safe."

"So I could be alone."

The silence hung heavy in the air. I couldn't even look at Mikah. Illy just stared at the table. Letting out a heavy sigh, he marched over to the door and opened it. "You have to understand, I loved you like you were my own children, but I never wanted to see you again. Go home. Forget your bloody vision, and forget about me."

Illy and I didn't look at each other. We knew what to do. She walked past Mikah without even a glance. I paused at the door and locked eyes with Mikah. A million emotions lingered on his face, but I lowered my head and walked out the door.

Illy went into the trees, walking as fast as she could. I called her name as I tried to keep up. She wouldn't stop. I grabbed her arm, and she whipped around to face me. "What?"

"What do we do now?" I asked.

"We go home," she said and looked up at the sky. She tried to hold it back, but a single tear left her eye and slid down her cheek.

"Illy," I said softly.

She looked back at me and laughed once, wiping at her eye. "I really thought we could do it. You, me, Mikah. Fight the Black Cloaks. Defeat them. I'm a fool."

"But you *saw*..."

She shook her head. "I must have been wrong."

I opened my mouth to say the obvious, but it wouldn't have helped. I didn't know what was true anymore.

So, we walked. It was late in the afternoon when we made it out of the forest. The bronze dragon came into view, but I didn't want to see it. I just wanted to keep going.

A strange noise hit my ears, but it was so far away I couldn't make it out. As it got closer, I heard the rapid thumps hitting the ground. A horse.

Illy turned first. "R-Raynor..."

I looked over my shoulder and saw the horse first, galloping toward us, a blur of ebony hair, and its rider draped in black. Behind him, a dozen people ran to keep up. Their black capes flowed behind them.

"RUN!" I shouted and grabbed Illy's hand. We took off, moving as fast as we could. I didn't know where we were going. I just knew we couldn't stop.

I held her hand as tight as I could. I heard our mother's last words to me: "Take care of your sister." They echoed in my ears as the hoof beats got louder and louder. Then something hard struck me across the back. We fell, and a sea of black surrounded us. Hands clawed at my arms. I held on so tight, but Illy was ripped away from me. They dragged us to our feet, two holding onto me, three struggling to hold Illy down as she thrashed about. The rest formed a half circle as the Cloak on the horse descended and walked toward us.

"So, it's true," he said, throwing his hood back to reveal a hideous grin on a pale face with dark, slicked-back hair. "A nice pair of twins just wandering around with no one to protect them."

How? How did they find us? How did they know we existed? "We're not twins," I said, but I knew my shaky voice would never convince him.

"Not twins?" he laughed, and the whole group laughed along. He pointed at Illy. "You cut the hair of this one, I'd swear you were the same person. Next you'll be telling me you aren't Gifted."

I looked right into his eyes. "We're *not*." I hoped the half-truth was enough.

The back of his hand came hard against my cheek. My head jerked to the side, but the two Cloaks held me steady. "You're a terrible liar, boy."

What could save us now—the truth or a lie? If they thought we were Gifted, they would take us, but if they thought we weren't, they would kill us. But we were twins—they had to be sure.

"He's not Gifted," Illy said. She stopped struggling.

I stared at her, wide-eyed. *No.*

"And what about you?" the leader asked, focusing his attention on her.

The corner of her mouth lifted into a smile. "I guess you'll have to find out."

I couldn't tell what she was doing. Maybe she wanted to keep them guessing. Maybe she thought she was protecting me. But how could she protect herself now?

The leader grinned as he stared at Illy. He snapped his fingers. "Bring him here," he said. Two people moved forward. I realized one person in the group wasn't wearing black.

The boy couldn't have been more than thirteen. His clothing was tattered and worn, and a chain was locked around his neck. One of the Cloaks held the other end like a leash. I knew instantly—the boy was a Tracker. Someone must have seen us, any one of the countless faces we'd come across on our journey. They'd known what we were, and they told the Black Cloaks, who must have been tracking us ever since. I hoped that stranger got a knife to his throat instead of a pocket full of gold.

The Cloak holding the chain pulled it, dragging the boy to him. The boy clawed at his neck as the chain pulled tighter. "Is this as far as they went?" the leader asked him.

The boy shook his head. "No," he choked, and his guard released the chain. The boy fell to his knees, coughing and spitting, but they kicked him until he stood again.

The leader of the group took a few steps forward. "All right," he said, pointing to the chain holder and the two Cloaks beside him. "You three, find out where they went. The rest of us will head back." He turned back to us. His wicked grin grew as he looked back and forth between me and my sister. "I want to see what these two can do."

The two groups parted, and we were dragged off so fast I could barely keep up. We'd feared this moment our entire lives, but right then, I could only think of Mikah. They would find him and kill him, all because we sought him out. He just wanted to be alone. At least we were going to live. I hoped.

After an hour or so, we reached a stone structure that seemed too large to be a house but too small to be a castle. Then I saw the bars on every window. The Cloaks unlocked a heavy, iron gate and led us inside. They dragged us through several dark rooms and down a long staircase. There were no windows in this room, only a few torches lining the walls. The Cloak holding me threw me onto the ground, and I watched helplessly as the group descended on Illy. They had shackled her wrists; the chains attached to them were bolted to the floor. Yet there she stood with her mouth stern and her head held high. She wouldn't break easy.

Once she was secure, most of the Cloaks filed back up the stairs and shut the door, all but one—the one I didn't want it to be. The man grinned as he looked at us, not sure where to start. "We could make this easy," he said, taking a step toward my sister. "You could just tell me what Gift you have, sweetheart." He grabbed her chin, but she yanked it away. She tried to spit in his face, but he took a step back and laughed. "You're a feisty one." He sighed as he walked calmly back and forth in front of Illy. "What about you, boy?" He turned toward me. "You want to tell me your sister's Gift? There's a great reward in it for you."

I stared at the floor.

"So, where's your Gift, then?" He nudged me with his foot. "If one of you is Gifted, then you both must be."

My eyes shot up. "I'm not," I insisted, staring him down.

He looked back and forth between us. A puzzled look crinkled his eyebrows. "You sure you're twins?" Lying about that now was pointless, so I said nothing. "No matter," he said. "I'll get it out of you. One way or another."

He lifted his foot again and kicked me hard on the thigh. "Get up!" I saw Illy's face as I stood—still strong and emotionless. The Cloak grabbed the back of my neck and pushed me forward, and then he moved behind me and pushed something cold and hard against my throat. Illy's stone face crumbled.

"How many pieces would you like your brother in?" He pressed the blade into my skin, and I shut my eyes. I hoped it would be quick.

"No, wait, don't! I'm a Seer!"

I opened my eyes as he lowered the dagger from my throat. *No*, I thought. I wasn't worth it. And it wouldn't save me.

The Cloak pushed me aside. "A Seer? What a lucky day. We don't have one of those." He stepped over to her and grabbed her chin. "How about you give us a nice vision, love?"

"It doesn't work that way, you idiot."

"No?" he asked. He lifted the dagger and tapped it against her cheek. "Well, I have more than a few ways to motivate you." With the knife still pressed to her skin, he put his lips on hers. She tried to pull back, but he slid the dagger down to her throat.

Rage boiled deep within my gut, and I clenched my fists. I saw him touch her, felt the sickening dread of his grin. I thought of every possible way he could hurt my sister and all I saw was my anger—a bright, red-hot flame.

"STOP!" I screamed and opened my hands. A fire twice as tall as me erupted out of nowhere and swept up the Cloak's back, consuming that terrible cape and his body with it. He shouted and thrashed. The orange flames clung to him until he fell to the ground. The fire vanished, but the heat of it radiated from my hands. I stared in horror at the charred corpse at my feet; his skin now as black as his cloak. I looked up at my sister.

"Fire," Illy said. Her eyes were wide with realization.

My whole body shook. The palms of my hands felt hot, but it didn't hurt. It hadn't hurt for a second.

Illy stood there, her jaw trembling as her mouth hung open. She tugged on the chains holding her. "Get these off me!" she screamed and pulled with no results. "Raynor, get me out of these things!"

I peered around and saw a key hanging on the wall. I grabbed it and unlocked the shackles from my sister's wrists. The chains clattered to the floor, and she threw her arms around me.

"How?" It was the only word that came to mind.

Illy took a step back and punched me on the arm. "I told you so!"

The realization didn't come to me right away. I couldn't understand, couldn't accept it. I looked down at the fallen Cloak and felt the heat tingling on my hands. That fire hadn't just appeared. I made it. I had to protect my sister; it was the only way I could ever want to be Gifted.

Illy smiled up at me, but I couldn't be happy yet. I'd killed one Cloak, but there were dozens more upstairs, and I didn't know how or if I could make that fire again. How were we going to escape?

Then we heard the screams. We jumped at the first one—long, deep, unexpected. More screams followed. The more joining the chorus, the more frantic they became. The rapid footsteps sounded like thunder above our heads. A loud thump, and another—so many I lost count. Then silence.

"What just happened?" Illy asked.

"I...I don't know." I just knew that we had to get out. I took her hand, and we went up the stairs, clinging to the wall in the darkness. I opened the door, ready to attack or run.

The smell hit me first—a mixture of smoke, the putrid sting of burnt fabric, and something else—an unsettling resemblance to burnt meat. We moved into the room, and I grabbed Illy to shield her eyes from the sight of it. She ripped away. She wasn't afraid. Their burnt bodies littered the floor—every last one of them. I felt horrified, yet relieved. We were going to escape.

"Did you...?" Illy asked.

I shook my head. "No. I couldn't have."

"Bloody Cloaks," a voice grumbled.

I pushed Illy aside, ready to fight, until Uncle turned the corner.

"There now, see what you've done?" Mikah scolded us. "Got yourselves snatched up by Cloaks, and then they come after *me*. Now I had to burn all those buggers to a crisp."

Illy's mouth fell open. "*You* burned them?"

"Well, they sure as hell didn't do it to themselves."

"*You* have a fire gift?"

He stared at us like we were crazy. "Obviously. Why?"

I looked at Illy then back at Mikah. "Because fire just burst out of my hands and killed the Cloak downstairs."

Mikah blinked a few times, then folded his arms across his chest. "Of course, it did. And I suppose you'll want me to train you? Come on."

We left the prison. I had so many questions, but right then I was just glad to be free and safe. There would be time to sort out all the rest later.

"I've never heard of a fire gift," Illy said. "What do

you call it?"

"I don't call it anything," Mikah said.

"Well, you'll have to now. You're not the only one."

I stopped and grabbed Illy's arm. "We can worry about that later." I pointed. A line of black came toward us slowly, even more Cloaks than before. My heart thumped in fear, but then it changed to something else. Excitement.

Mikah grabbed Illy's arm and moved her against the wall. "You stay there. Try not to have a vision unless it's important."

She smiled as she looked at us. Her eyes gleamed. "I already had it. A long time ago."

Mikah stepped forward, and I followed him. We stood side by side as the wall of Cloaks came closer. "Don't feel right, going into battle without a sword."

"You have something better," I said.

"We both do."

Mikah held out his open palms, and two bright balls of orange fire appeared in his hands. He looked at me and smiled.

I held out my hands and felt the heat rise.

The End

Sarah Foster is a blogger and an aspiring novelist and poet. She lives with her stand-up comedian husband and an overweight cat in a studio apartment above a movie theater just south of Boston, Massachusetts. When she's not obsessing over Broadway musicals or baking cupcakes, she is usually working on finishing—and hopefully someday publishing—her debut novel. You can read about her writing adventures (and the love/hate relationships with her characters) on her blog, The Faux Fountain Pen.

THE LAST DRAGON

www.thefauxfountainpen.blogspot.com
www.twitter.com/Sarah_A_Foster

Mind Body Soul
By Elizabeth Seckman

She was his queen.

Had been since she was but a girl of sixteen.

He knew she never loved him. She'd married him out of duty to her people. She was from the Southern Shores, a land battered by invaders from the Plains. It was her union with the King of the Mountains, and his fierce army of warriors that brought an end to the violence.

In return, she brought his people a different sort of peace. The people of the Southern Shores were poets and artisans, and they shared their gifts with the people of the Mountains. Until the Queen's arrival, the Mountain people's only art was crafting of swords so perfect, their edges sliced through bone like butter without ever losing their shine.

As a tranquil complacency settled over the land, the now-idle King had time to sit on his throne and think.

His queen was still lovely. The years had been kinder to her than to him. The scars on his face were hidden by the deep grooves chiseled into his features by worry. That same worry turned his dark hair a silvery gray. His queen's hair still fell down her back in raven waves; her skin as smooth and unmarred as the day they married.

As he contemplated their situation, she turned to him and smiled, like she knew his thoughts were turned to her.

Loyal. Devoted. That was his queen.

Not once had she followed her heart. Not even

when their union produced no heir did she leave him, or stray from the marriage bed.

"Your Highness, is there a response?"

The king snorted. "I'll have to take this matter under consideration. Tell no one of this."

"But your Highness—the queen. Were not she and Lord Billings quite...close...in their youth?"

The squire's words were like an irritating gald to the King's ears. "Do you dare lecture me on the friendships of my Queen? Shall I vacate my throne and let you sit here and tell me what to do? Grab your sword. I dare you try."

The young squire took a step back, caught his foot on thin air and stumbled to the floor. Not making any move to stand, he addressed his king with lowered eyes and a quiver in his voice, "No, your majesty. I presume too much."

"Get up and get out." The king stood, his wolf fur cloak hanging heavy on his back. With a nod to his queen, he turned and made his way to his private chamber. The dank stone hallway with its stale cool air was a welcomed relief to the warmth of the great hall where fires blazed in the hearths from whatever dinner was planned for whichever royalty meandered through the area and needed to be entertained.

"My Lord," the queen said, her small feet making no noise as she moved quickly around him until she blocked his path. "Are you feeling unwell?"

"I am...feeling a bit under the weather and could use a night to rest. Does that cause you any grievance?"

"Of course not, My Lord. I shall call for Mrs. O'Shay."

"No, no," he said with a shake of his burly head. "No need for that. Perhaps Modesto has a draught that could be of use."

"That old sorcerer? I should say not. I would never

allow him to minister to the hounds in the courtyard, much less my king."

The king smiled. Taking her hand, so small in his big palm, almost like a child's. He pulled it to his lips and kissed it. "You have always been the most worthy of queens."

"As you have been the most worthy of kings."

"I hope that is so," he said with a frown.

"Of course it is so. You have saved my people, brought prosperity and peace to the lands."

"The protection and contentment of his subjects is the foremost duty of a king."

"Only the good ones, My Lord," she said with a smile, giving his hand a small squeeze. "I suppose," she said, adjusting his cloak, pulling the soft fur closed across his barrel-like chest. "You can have tonight to rest. When the festivities get merry and no one is paying any mind to me, I'll slip away and bring you some tea."

"That would be much appreciated, My Queen."

They stood in the hallway for several moments. She...clutching his cloak, and he...wishing he had the nerve to kiss her good-bye.

A door opened and a servant girl dressed in gray with a white cap curtsied low and said to the Queen. "Your Ladyship, Bishop Bauer would like you to be present for the blessing."

"But of course." The queen smiled up at her king, giving his cheek a gentle pat. "You rest." Then she let go of his cloak and followed the servant down the long hall.

***

"I didn't bloody ask for a lecture. I asked you if it could be done," the King demanded of the small man with wisps of wild, wiry black hair.

"It is dark magic. Can it be done is NOT the question

you should be asking. The question is SHOULD it be done? Tomorrow, I will—"

"I don't have time for philosophical debate. A courier arrived this evening. Lord Billings is dying. His life force is down to hours, not days."

"Making what you propose all the more preposterous. Why would you trade bodies with a dying man?"

"It is what the Queen deserves. Lord Billings was her betrothed. The love of her youth. She married me to save a kingdom, nothing more. And together, we've done that. Our world is at peace. She has shown me more love than a bastard like myself deserves. I want her to understand the same happiness she has brought me."

"You'll be giving him everything. Your body. Your wife. Your kingdom. It's utter madness."

"They say love makes a man go a little soft in the head, perhaps it is true. This is what I want, Modesto. Make it happen or I'll spend the rest of my days finding different ways to torture you."

Pressed so tight, the sorcerer's think lips drew into a near invisible line, but with a shake of his head, he told the king what to gather for the spell.

* * *

The merry-makers clamored for more ale and more songs, not the company of their monarch, so the queen quietly excused herself. As she made her way from the hall, Count Driscoll stopped her with a gentle hand on her forearm. "Your majesty, might I have a word?"

"But of course," she said, her smile hiding her annoyance at the delay. It was an odd thing for her king to be ill. In all their years of marriage, he had never once complained, not even the time gangrene had set in his calf from a battle wound.

"Lord Billings has fallen gravely ill. At first they

thought it was a bit of the dropsy, but it seems to be consuming him. When I left Southern Shores this morning, his breathing was so labored, I doubt I shall ever see him alive again."

"Oh dear," the Queen said, gripping a chair rail for support. "William and I were the best of childhood friends. Are you certain of this diagnosis?"

"Yes, My Lady."

Closing her eyes a moment, she seemed to be drumming up the strength to accept the news. It only took her a few seconds to square her chin and nod to Count Driscoll. "I shall send our regards to his family. You will keep me apprised of their needs? I should hate to find them wanting...his family was always very dear to me."

"Of course, My lady."

The queen nodded and continued to make her way out of the hall, down the dank corridor, and to her husband's chamber.

Laughter could be heard through the heavy oak door. The queen's brow dipped and she frowned. It was not like her king to be so—boisterous. Pressing her ear closer, she listened. The laughter, the voice was as familiar to her as her own.

It was her husband's voice. But something was terribly wrong.

Trepidation in her gut made her hand feel as heavy and cold as the iron handle she pressed to swing the door open. Her heart did a stutter-beat at the sight.

Her husband, the king, a man with a spine stiffened by honor and a demeanor made serious by the weight of duty was...jumping on the bed?

Like a small, excitable child, he was holding onto the thick canopy pole as he bounced at the knees on the feather mattress. The queen took a suck of breath. Was he suffering a fever? A madness?

"Mellow Dee, my love! Can you believe it? Can you

believe the gods have smiled upon me?"

Mellow Dee? No, no, she thought. "Where is he? Where is that black guard, Modesto?"

The jubilant king slid off the bed, moving toward her with a slyness in his smile that made her take a step back toward the door.

"It's fate, Mel, don't you understand? Fate knew we should be together. I remained faithful to you...in my heart...and I, nay we have been rewarded."

"What reward is this? Where is my husband?"

The jubilant king frowned as he shrugged off the fur cloak, allowing it to gather on the floor. The queen scooped it up, brushing the fur gently as she laid the cloak reverently over the velvet-topped bench at the foot of the bed.

"I would assume he is in my dying body. I mean, if I am here—"

"No! No, no, no. This will not do. This must be put to rights. It was the sorcerer. I'll have him hanged by his feet and flogged with willow whips." Her rant continued a she bolted from the chamber, running through the hallway.

The Jubilant King was right behind her. Grabbing her arm, he spun her toward him. "This is our chance. We can finally be together, like we were when we were young."

She yanked her arm from his grip. Her eyes narrowed; her head shaking, "I am not some girl. I am the queen, the wife of Edgar Lyall, King of the Mountain."

"Well then, it's your lucky day. Seems I am the new and improved Edgar. Together we can rule this kingdom. You and I."

"Unhand me. This must be undone."

"Perhaps you haven't noticed, but I am now the king."

"Imposter," she yelled, but her words echoed

impotently through the empty hall.

"You can spend your time undoing magic or you can go. Go find your king. If memory serves me well, and it does, I can assure you, he is a few painful breaths away from leaving this earth forever."

A sound that was part sob, part gasp slipped from her parted lips. It only took her a moment to gather her wits and her skirts and run through the castle halls to the stables. The stable hands, shocked by the sudden appearance of their queen, dropped the rakes and shovels they were using to clean the stalls and bowed.

"No time for that. Prepare me a horse."

"A horse, your majesty?" the elder of the hands asked. "Are you planning to ride at this hour of night? Alone?"

"No. I do not. I intend to go to Southern Shores, and I want to make haste. Stop dallying and do as I asked."

"Your highness, if I might suggest a carriage? Billy, crack snappy," the elder hand said with a snap of his fingers. "Awaken Donovan and tell him the queen needs a driver. Gerald, put away your rake, you and I will have to do as footman." The elder footman bowed. "Kenny LeWayne, at your service, my queen. We'll get you home safe and sound. Have no fears on that."

The queen's mouth pulled into a tight bow. "That's not my home, but thank you. Your service will not be forgotten. If you would, Billy, please alert Mrs. O'Shay, too. I need her to come along."

* * *

Kenny sat across from her, peaking from the curtain-covered windows as he gripped the revolver in his lap. The carriage was making good time since they had emerged from the dense climbs of the mountains for the flat land of the coast. Mrs. O'Shay muttered with every bump, but said nothing intelligible.

The queen rested her head against the carriage seat until the inky darkness began to turn grey. "I need to get to Balfour Castle," she said as the sun started to glow in the horizon lighting up the once-familiar land.

"Balfour, My lady?" Mrs. O'Shay asked. Kenny's brow raised, but he said nothing.

They know, the queen thought.

Truth was every subject in her kingdom knew the tale of how she was smitten with love for the lord with the face of a Greek God and the spirit of a mischievous nymph. The banners announcing their betrothal had been announced and the epic wedding was being planned when the young Lady Melody Grayson disappeared one day, only to reappear, wed to the barbaric king of the mountain realm. The logical and pragmatic members of the realm knew the union was a wise one. The Southern Shores needed the protection. Without it, they would have fallen to the Plains People—a nation of locusts—who moved in a swarm overwhelming and devouring nation after nation. The plains people had been mere miles from the Southern Shore borders.

With the might of the Mountain People and their allies the Free Nation, the swarm was not only pushed back, but scattered. Without unity, the Plains People were nothing to fear and a peace was brought to their small corner of the universe.

The young-girl queen's heart had broken in those early days. She missed her home. She missed the warmth of the sun and the smell of the salt on the breeze. Her new mountain home was cool and the damp air carried the smell of moss and fresh earth. And her new husband never smiled. Never joked. He was an old man of twenty-five. A warrior who couldn't dance and knew very little about manners of court and the graces of a king. His crown was earned in battle, not inherited through blood.

"Yes, Balfour," her words sharp. She could not explain, so she would not even try.

Kenny frowned. Mrs. O'Shay folded her arms over her plump chest and sniffed, but neither said a word.

* * *

The dying king took a labored breath. Only sheer will gave him the strength to sit up and face his queen. Sheer will, and possibly a bit of fear.

His sweet, gentle queen smashed a water crock against the wall above his head.

"Be calm, my lady," the king's words were raspy. "I never knew you to have such bad temper, or such horrible aim."

"I wasn't aiming for you. Had I wanted to bash you in your thick, stupid skull, I'd have done it." She pulled off her traveling gloves and stuffed them in her cloak before kneeling before him and taking his hand in hers. "What did you do?"

The king coughed. A wet rattle that took his breath away. Sweat beaded on his brow as he struggled to appear commanding and strong. "I gave you your life back."

"You gave me my life back?" The queen threw his words back at him, only much louder. "What has come over you? What insanity are you suffering? It was Modesto, wasn't it? He has put a spell on you."

"I requested—nay commanded the swap. I heard of Sir William's fate. That he had days to live. Your service to your kingdom is done. The lands are at peace. You deserved—"

"I deserved to be consulted about my life. Did you think you just had the right, the authority, to choose the path of my life?"

"You loved William."

"Pah. I was but a girl, and girls know nothing of love."

"You shed tears when you left him."

"I was a girl...leaving my home, my family... everything I knew for a new life. A life I want to keep."

The king offered no response. With a sigh, she ordered, "Lie back."

"I—"

"Lie back," she repeated with a gentle push to his shoulders. Once his back was settled onto the bed, she lifted his legs and shoved them back under the down covers. "You will rest. Mrs. O'Shay will minister to you and we'll try to keep you alive long enough to undo this madness."

The queen turned to Mrs. O'Shay, who cowered against the wall with wide-eyes. "Your majesty, I don't understand..."

The queen frowned as she explained. "It seems my dear husband has chosen to play clairvoyant and decide he knows what's in my heart and my head. But like any thick-skulled, short-sighted male, he has made a mess of things. Swapping souls with a dying man. I swear to the All-Mighty, I never dreamed he'd do anything so rash...so stupid."

"But, but...how?" Mrs. O'Shay looked as pale and frightened as if she was in the room with demons and devils.

"Modesto. Tinkering with black magic—which is forbidden in the realm. He will pay—"

Mrs. O'Shay grabbed the queen by the arm. "But my lady, it's impossible. You abandoned your husband...you might be committing treason, or worse...adultery."

"I know my husband, Mrs. O'Shay. I can't be fooled by a swap of skin and bone. But you bring up a good point. I will be judged harshly for abandoning my king and kingdom for a dying love from my past." The queen tucked the blankets around the king firmly as she talked. "You've put me in a predicament, My

Lord. I hope you're quite satisfied with yourself."

The king's eyes pressed closed and he took a tired breath. "No, my lady, I am not at all satisfied that you are not pleased."

"Truly? Not even a bit?"

The king's smile was weak, but genuine. "I am greatly pleased you are not satisfied with the change."

"Good." She placed a kiss on his forehead, allowing her lips to linger against the sweat-coated skin. A tear slid down her cheek, but she swiped it away. Clearing her throat as she stood, she said to the medicine woman, "I'll leave him in your capable hands. Please, whatever it takes, keep him alive until I can get Modesto to undo this spell."

"Yes, my lady." Mrs. O'Shay gathered her bags and set them on the dresser top and began pulling out bottles and bags of medicines and herbs.

The queen, content that the king was in capable hands, gave her husband another kiss and hurried from the room in a swish of skirts.

She made her way to the stables. Lord William's sister, Capernia, met her in the hall. "My Lady," Lady Capernia said. "I cannot believe—why if I had known you'd visit...I'd have—"

"No time for that. No red carpets or trumpets needed. I am here as a friend. Perhaps I have brought some help that can save or at least prolong my—Lord William's life."

"Oh, well, I hate for you to waste your time. Or expend unnecessary energy. Father called in all the best doctors. They are certain there is no cure."

"They're not Mrs. O'Shay. The woman can work miracles."

"Really?" Carpenia asked with a frown.

The queen halted her steps. "You sound disappointed."

Redness rose from Capernia's chest to her cheeks.

Her hands fiddled nervously with the silk of her gown. "No, of course not. I just hate to get, um, false hope."

"We'll do our best. We just need peace and quiet... can we be assured of that?"

"Of peace and quiet?"

The queen nodded.

"Most certainly. It's not like Lord William has any visitors but myself, and you of course, My Lady. What he lacks in numbers, he makes up for in quality."

The queen's brow arched, but she said nothing more. She thanked Capernia and moved quickly to the stables. There, she directed the carriage driver and footman to return to the castle and bring back Modesto—with a tip of a blade to his heart if need be. The men made arrangements for fresh horses to be hitched to the carriage and they were off.

The queen made her way back to her husband.

He was sleeping peacefully. Mrs. O'Shay had a pot of menthol simmering next to a now-roaring fire. The room was so warm, the queen shrugged out of her cloak before settling herself on a chair next to his bed.

"I've given him a few potions. And a salve to his chest. He seems a mite better already."

"Blessings on you, good woman," the queen said, giving the woman's plump hand a squeeze. "I am forever in your debt."

"He really is the king, isn't he My lady?"

The queen smiled. "Aye. I would recognize that spirit if it was slid into a fox."

"Why would he, My lady? Why would he do such an insane thing?"

The queen sighed. "I was once betrothed to Lord William. He was the love of my young heart. He could make me laugh with his good humor, and my how he could dance. There wasn't a reel he didn't know."

"And now, My lady?"

HERO LOST: MYSTERIES OF DEATH AND LIFE

"Now? My dear Mrs. O'Shay, age brings wisdom, and a wise heart chooses its prey by much more judiciously than a young, foolish heart. It only took me a year with the king to know he was a rare man. His noble heart is fair and reasonable. His generosity is without match. He is as brave as a lion, yet tender as a kitten. I can find no other to take his place." A silent, hot tear slid down her cheek.

Mrs. O'Shay gave her a reverent head nod. "I will do my best, My Lady. I believe I can surely keep him alive and breathing for as long as it takes the men to fetch Modesto."

The queen gave her a smile. "You should go rest. I'll sit with him. This chamber has a twin room through that door. These were mother and father's quarters. We'd often stay here during the Jubilation."

Mrs. O'Shay offered only a few words of argument. It wasn't befitting a nurse maid to argue with her queen. "Wake me if there are any concerns," Mrs. O'Shay said, as she backed out of the room, closing the door between the two chambers.

Once the room grew silent, save for the crackling of the fire, the queen listened closely to her husband's steady breaths. After a few hours, her eyelids started to droop. Shaking off the tiredness, she rose and tended the fire, bringing it back to a roar before adding a few more logs.

"Come," the king whispered. "Come lay with me."

"You need to rest," she said, standing straight, trying to flex the tightness from her muscles.

"I need to be close to my wife."

The queen opened her mouth as if there was more argument to come, but she closed it and crawled into bed next to him. She wrapped her arms around him and brushed kisses against his temple.

"I'm feeling some regret, my queen."

"Some?"

MIND BODY SOUL

"Yes, some. The only satisfaction I have procured from this decision is the knowledge that I have won your heart. That I am not ranked among the mistakes in your life."

"You are far from a mistake. You are my world."

"But I gave you no heirs."

"Nay, I gave you no heirs," she corrected. She nestled closer to a foreign body made familiar by his soul, and said, "Though as far as I am concerned, we are enough."

* * *

When the small envoy to the mountain castle returned, their news was not good.

In the thirty-six hours it took them to travel there and back, Modesto was nowhere to be found and a the Mountain Kingdom was on the brink of war.

"War?!" The queen spat the words.

"Yes, My Lady, war."

"I've only been gone a few days. Lord William has only reigned for a night—how in the All Mighty's name could we be on the brink of war?"

"It seems, your Highnesss, that the King, err Lord William, had himself a party and invited royalty from every court."

"And how did that come to war?"

"Once the good lord was deep in his cups, he made an advance on Queen Isabella of the Low Lands. Her king was offended and quick to challenge the king to a duel. The queen of the Plains stepped in to cool the tempers of the men, but Lord William assured her that his bed was open to her as well, though she was a bit plump and not nearly as comely as Isabella."

The queen's face glowed red and her clenched jaw twitched. "You mean to tell me lives are to be lost because William has the libido and sensibilities of a fifteen-year-old peasant?"

"T'would seem, your majesty."

The growl that emerged from the queen's lips was not at all regal. In a flounce of fabric, she went about the room tackling the chore of packing her bags with venom. "I suppose I must return. I must stop William. I must find Modesto. I can't trust that anything can be done that I don't do myself."

The carriage driver twisted his wool hat in his hands. "I'm sorry, My lady."

"Ohhh, it's not your fault. It's my husband's. Don't you think that he won't get an earful once he's got his ears firmly planted on his own head."

"I...uh..."

"Go rest, Mr. Thomas. I'll speak with Calpernia and see if she will lend me a team of horses and drivers."

"I can make the trip, your highness. The men and I, we took turns sleeping and driving. We're still fit to transport and protect our queen."

"Well then, please ready the horses and the men. I'll say farewell to my husband and we'll be on our way."

The queen said her reluctant good-byes to her husband, leaving him in the capable hands of Mrs. O'Shay.

The ride back was unnerving. The queen spent most of it staring out the coach window. This time, she paid no mind to the scenery. Her mind was devoted to planning. Should she play nice to William and find a covert way to return his rot-gut soul to his own body? Or should she be firm and demand to know where Modesto was?

Reason quickly told her to play nice. William had the brain capacity of a horny rabbit—certainly manipulating him shouldn't be hard.

As the carriage pulled into the castle stables, the trumpets sounded to alert the castle to the return of the queen. From every corridor and shadowy alley, people poured into the court yard. The queen rolled up her curtains and waved to her people as she passed.

At the center of the courtyard square, a wide staircase led to the Royal Hall where the king sat on his throne and listened to public grievances and official cases. As the carriage slowed to a stop, the king emerged, looking very regal in his royal robes.

The queen took a breath. Gone was her husband's modest fur cloak, replaced by a shimmering silk of scarlet. The queen swallowed her distaste and braced herself for her ruse.

The footman opened the door to her carriage, ushering her out.

On shaking legs, she made her way to the king. Once she was within striking distance, she held out her hand and said, "My dear King. How handsome you look in your new finery."

The king sneered. "Seems the reality of the situation has finally settled in and given you sensible thoughts."

"Indeed," she said, offering him a smile.

"Excellent," he said as he pulled her close. "I have been waiting a lifetime for this."

His mouth plundered hers. She closed her eyes and reminded herself that it was for the greater good, but as one hand pulled her tighter, his other slid down over the curve of her hip to cup her bottom. She blamed instinct for what happened next.

In one fluid movement, she shoved him away with one hand and slapped him across the face with the other.

The king's reaction was just as swift. He grabbed her arm and twisted it behind her back, holding her against him as he called for his guards. His men—so loyal, so blind—bound her arms and legs and practically dragged her to the dungeon.

"He's not my husband, you fools. How can you

not see it?"

She screamed. Unable to strike at them with her hands or feet, she tried to goad them with words. They never even flinched. Probably too stupid to comprehend.

The iron gate of the dungeon creaked open.

"Perhaps a day or two in a dark hole will bring you to your sense, your highness."

"A pox on you, you idiotic dog."

He shoved her in the cell, causing her to fall, her cheek scraping against the stone floor.

As she struggled to right herself, a hand reached out and grabbed her by the elbow. She jerked away.

"Tis all right, My lady. It is me, Modesto. Allow me to help you."

"Modesto? You damned fool—of course you will help me. Untie me and then you must undo this madness."

Cold, soft hands loosened the rope that bound her hands. Once her hands were free, she began work on her legs. "You must return my husband to his body."

"Don't you think if I could do that, I already would have?"

"What do you mean—you can't?"

"I do not have what I need to make the magic work, and I am certain the new king won't supply me with the ingredients."

"Perhaps we could bribe a guard? There has to be one here who is loyal to my husband."

"Few have caught on. Those who have are locked up here with us."

"No, I will not accept that. What do you need? I'll get it."

Modesto laughed. It was more like a sarcastic puff of air through his nose, but it was how the man showed humor. "I need something that belongs to both men. Something personal."

"What did you use to cast the first spell?"

"A love letter from William to you and the king's wedding band."

The queen grimaced. "It wasn't a love letter. It was a—"

"It doesn't matter the content. It was script written by his own hand."

The queen started patting her pockets, as if searching for something. Then her gaze landed on her hand. "What about my wedding ring? The king gave it to me. And this," she plucked a hair from her shoulder. "This could be Lord William's."

"I don't know. I suppose there is no harm in trying." Modesto strung the hair through gold ring and started his chant.

Nothing.

The queen's heart pounded and her mouth went dry as she prayed the switch could be reversed.

The ring hung limp from the strand of hair.

Tears burned her eyes. Her husband would die alone and she would spend the rest of her days in this dungeon. The first tear fell, followed by another. She didn't bother to wipe them away. What need was there for strength? For dignity? All that she loved was lost.

Modesto continued to chant.

Nothing.

"Are you certain you remember the spell?"

"Of course, I remember the spell. It's just...well, how do you even know this is a strand of William's hair? And the ring is yours, not the king's. You can't blame me for obvious flaws—"

Modesto quieted. He cupped the ring and hair in his hand moved them closer to the queen's stomach.

"What is it?" she asked.

Modesto closed his eyes and chanted louder. The queen felt a warmth in her belly. The warmth grew, seemed to take a shape, like an effervescent ball of energy.

"My lady, did you happen to—you and the king, err, William?"

The queen gave him a forceful push that sent the thin man to the floor.

"I hardly think that is any of your business." As she spoke the words, the energy in her stomach grew, causing her to feel as if she was falling in a dream. Clutching the stone wall behind her, she let out a gasp as the energy emerged in a misty ball the size of a bumble bee. It circled the cell a few times and then zipped through the bars and was gone.

"A child. The creation from the body of William and the soul of the king."

"A child?" The queen wrapped a protective hand over her belly. "But what of my husband? Did it work?"

Modesto righted himself, brushing off the filth from the floor. "Only time will tell, My Lady."

Minutes passed. The queen stood, pacing the small cell. Modesto sat in the corner, luring in a rat with a crust of bread.

"How can you just sit there? You have to have some way of knowing whether or not your spell worked."

The dungeon doors flew open, the creak of the iron hinges echoing off the stone walls. A huge figure carrying a torch lumbered into the place, stopping at the cell door.

It was the king.

He looked upon his queen with eyes glazed with tears. "Open this door," he yelled to the jailer.

The queen smiled. When the door opened, she held out her hand to the king who gripped it in his big paw, kissing the palm before pressing it to his heart. "Come, My Queen. We have a war to stop and a kingdom to set to rights."

MIND BODY SOUL

Collapsing against his chest, she dried her tears against the silk of his tunic. He held her a few minutes, neither speaking until the queen stiffened her spine and said with a faux-smirk, "Be forewarned, My King. You will be hearing of this folly of yours and Modesto's for as long as we live."

"I pray that is many, many years," the king said with a grateful smile.

"I don't know, My Queen," Modesto said, scurrying to her side. "Call it crazy, but my magic has provided the kingdom with an heir."

The End

Elizabeth is a multi-published author of women's fiction and romance. The mother of four boys, five if you count their father, she needs all the fantasy girl time she can get. A graduate of Marshall University, she is a licensed social worker who spent years working with at-risk teens. She is a member of WV Writers Association and an active blogger.
Facebook: www.facebook.com/eseckmanbooks/
Author blog: www.eseckman.blogspot.com/
Group Blog: www.reallyrealhousewivesofamerica.blogspot.com/

Captain Bulat
By Olga Godim

"Milord." Altenay sprang to her feet as the opulently dressed older man with thick silver hair, Councilor Shamer, entered her office. Two bodyguards with hard, pitiless eyes accompanied him.

"You're the Finder? You find things and people?"

His beautiful baritone would do wonders on stage, Altenay thought irreverently. What did the city's most popular councilor want with her? "Yes, Milord," she replied softly. Finding things was her business, but she hadn't worked for any nobleman since she started a year ago. Her clients were tradesmen and farmers. She didn't aspire any higher. Her magic was small, and she hadn't earned her magician guild's license yet. How had he even heard about her?

"I want you to find someone," he said, his patrician features cold. His gaze swept over her face and figure, her long dark braids, and her red ornate tubeteika, the customary headgear for many Bessar women. His lips curled, as if being in her tiny establishment, conversing with her, was beneath him.

She bristled at his derision but she couldn't afford to alienate him. One of the most powerful men in the city, he could destroy her with a word. She bent her head, and the faint chiming of the tiny coins fringing her tubeteika calmed her. She bit her tongue on a sharp retort and replied civilly.

"Who do you wish me to find, Milord?"

"You're younger than I thought," he said. He studied her tubeteika with disfavor. "I want you to find Captain Bulat."

CAPTAIN BULAT

"Bulat?" Altenay racked her brain. The councilor pronounced it as if she should recognize the name, and she did, vaguely, but she couldn't recall the specifics. "Does he work for you?"

He snorted. "No. He was a hero of the last war. He and his brigade liberated this city from the oppressors but he disappeared shortly after the final victory. The City Council want to put up a memorial in his honor. A statue." He looked suddenly as if he bit into something sour.

"Oh." Altenay frowned. "But it was..." She calculated rapidly. "Twenty-five years ago."

"Quite," he said.

"You think he is still alive?"

"That's for you to find out." He tossed a fat purse on her desk, and the coins in the purse clinked merrily. "I believe that will cover your fees."

Altenay put her hands behind her back. She didn't want to touch the purse; it radiated poison, as if contaminated by his disdain, both for her and for the unknown Bulat. She could imagine a few compelling reasons why the man would've wanted to disappear and stay that way. "What if I can't find him? It was long ago."

"The way I heard it, you haven't met with a failure yet. Don't start with me."

The undisguised threat laced his voice. The man really wanted to find this Bulat captain, but she couldn't promise anything. Her magic might not work after so many years.

"Milord," she ventured. "Perhaps it would be better if you asked a more experienced magician. I only just started this business. So far, I've found a misplaced necklace, a stolen donkey, and a missing wagon, all lost within a very short time. I found purloined sandals once, but your request is for a human being. What if the man is dead?"

HERO LOST: MYSTERIES OF DEATH AND LIFE

His shapely mouth twisted. "Then bring me proof of his death."

Altenay sighed. He was set on his course. For some reason, he didn't wish to ask any of the established magic workers, and his next words confirmed her guess.

"I expect full discretion," he said. "You're not to talk about it to anyone and you report directly to me."

Alarm bells clamored in Altenay's head. This was some shady dealing, but she didn't have a choice. She couldn't refuse outright. "Of course, Milord," she said, knowing that she wouldn't keep this promise. "I'll tell no one and I'll do my best, but to find a man I need something that belonged to him. That's how my Finder's magic works. The longer the time he owned that thing, the higher my chances of success."

"Yes, they said so," he muttered. "Will this do?" He produced a dagger in an elaborate bronze sheath studded with gems. "Bulat owned this dagger for years but he left it behind when he disappeared."

"Nobody else used it afterwards?"

"No."

Altenay picked up the dagger and unsheathed it. Briefly, she brushed her fingers over the gems on the sheath and then along the deadly blade, not searching in truth, just experimenting. The pull of her magic was faint but unmistakable, although it dispersed like a mist. It seemed to tug her in several directions at once. Not a good sign. She needed to think about this one.

"Will it work?" he repeated his question.

"Possibly. It's worth a try. Thank you, Milord," she said.

"How long will it take?"

"I don't know. It might involve some traveling and some false leads. The first result might be wrong. It might take me to his old belt buckle, because the dagger hung on that belt."

He winced.

"I'm sorry, Milord. Magic is not a precise science. At least, my magic isn't. What do I do if I find him? Do I tell him you're looking? Or if I don't find him? How do I contact you?"

"Don't tell him anything," he snarled, but instantly moderated his tone. "I want it to be a surprise for him. Send a message to my mansion on the Hill."

"Of course, Milord," Altenay said meekly.

Long after he strode out, his bodyguards at his heels, she sat unmoving, staring at the wall of her office. Why the secrecy? The arrogant nobleman obviously had something nefarious in mind, but how did it concern her? And what about Captain Bulat? Did the City Council really want to honor him for his heroic deeds during the war? Or was it something more sinister?

The coins in the purse were all gold, more than she had ever owned in her entire life. Definitely something sinister, she thought morosely. Being involved in anything with so much money at stake made her stomach ache. Much safer to search for a stolen silver spoon for a few coppers. She wished the councilor had never found his way to her door.

After a while, when nobody else came in to distract her from her unhappy contemplations, she went through the connecting door to the workshop of her friend and roommate Vasilisa, to seek advice.

"Hi, Vasi, are you busy?" Altenay eyed Vasilisa's current work with suspicion. The creature emerging from her friend's skilled hands looked like nothing she had ever seen, a mix between a rabbit and a snake. As the youngest taxidermist in the city, Vasilisa often accepted weird jobs every other taxidermist refused. "What is this thing?"

"An escapee from an adventurous sorcerer,"

Vasilisa said absently, bending her freckled face over her work. "It's a construct. It escaped the sorcerer's lab and sought life on its own." She snorted. "And drowned in a puddle for its trouble. The sorcerer wants it mounted."

Altenay giggled and pulled at her friend's short russet braid. She liked the honey color and the silky texture of Vasilisa's hair much better than her own coarse black tresses. "Look at me. I have a question for you."

"I can work and talk at the same time. Your customer left?"

"My customer was Councilor Shamer with his bodyguards."

Vasilisa lifted her eyes from the odd creature in her hands. "Himself? What did he want?"

"He wants me to find a Captain Bulat, who disappeared right after the end of the war."

"The war? But it ended before we were born."

"Yes. He gave me a purse with more golden coins than both of us could earn in a year. And he swore me to secrecy."

"That's why you're talking to me?"

"Vasi, something is off in his request. Nothing legit costs so much. And why the secrecy?"

"You might be right," Vasilisa said slowly. "It might've been better if you didn't take the job. We don't need his money. We're doing well."

"I know. I tried. He wouldn't take 'No' for an answer. I need information before I start the search. Who was this Captain Bulat?"

Vasilisa shrugged. "I think he was some kind of a hero. It had to do with the siege of the city by the Sultan's army. But it was long ago. Maybe some older people remember?"

"I don't want to ask around. The councilor might hear about it. He would be displeased if I broke his secrecy code. I don't think it's a good idea to invoke his displeasure. The man was so cold, he gave me the willies. I don't think he liked my tubeteika." She flicked the coins hanging from the edge of the small cap. "Or me."

"Then he is a fool," Vasilisa said serenely. "I like your tubeteika. And you. And I'm no fool."

Altenay laughed. "That's for sure. But you don't know much about Captain Bulat."

"Nope. Sorry." Vasilisa resumed her work.

Altenay, grumbling her disappointment, retreated to her office. She would have to start her search with a very limited knowledge of her target, which didn't bode well for the results. She took a few deep breaths to access her inner calm, dropped cross-legged in the middle of the floor, and unsheathed the dagger again, caressing the ornate hilt and the austere gray steel of the blade with her finger. She let her magic flow in truth, but the blasted knife refused to divulge its former owner's location. Her magical pointer oscillated like a pendulum, swinging from wall to wall. Perhaps it would settle on one distinct direction if she crossed the city wall and divorced herself from the too dense swirl of humanity.

The next morning, she plaited her long dark hair into two thick braids, put on her favorite golden-cloth tubeteika, and stuffed the dagger into her traveling satchel.

"Good luck," Vasilisa said, as they hugged their goodbyes. "Be careful, will you? When are you coming back?"

Altenay shrugged. "I don't even know if I'm going anywhere, much less when I'll be back. I might come back in three hours. Or in three days. Don't fret, Vasi. I'll be fine. I hope the dagger will lead me somewhere."

That was the nature of her magic. To find anything, she had to follow her magic blindly and hope she wouldn't end up somewhere she couldn't handle. She made her way through the crowded streets to the northern edge of the city and the huge seaport. From there, she turned inland, following the city wall as best she could. Once in a while, she stopped to touch the dagger. The pull of her magic was stronger outside the walls, but the direction still wavered, although it leaned west. Of course, west was the logical choice. East of the city lay the sea.

Twice in the first couple hours of her journey, her eyes brushed across the same wiry man with a beard, dressed in the Council livery. He lingered a little behind her and both times slid out of sight before she took a good look. Did he know she carried the dagger? Did he hope to steal it? That would be odd—the Council servants were usually not thieves. Not in broad daylight anyway. Or did he follow her because he was in Councilor Shamer's employ? Or was he on an errant of his own? That was more probable. She didn't spot him again and eventually pushed him out of her mind.

The rain started soon after she left home, and by late afternoon, when she finally neared the end of her journey, the bustling river port, she was thoroughly wet and miserable. She still couldn't pinpoint her target.

The river wended its way from the southwest to the sea, and the city on the high northern shore guarded the sprawling delta. Across the river, on the southern shore, the swamps stretched all the way to the mountains, and behind those, lay the Sultanate, the kingdom's perpetual on-and-off enemy.

She tested the dagger numerous times during her trek around the city, but all in vain. Perhaps Bulat didn't wish to be found and was befuddling her magic on purpose. She would try again one last time. If it didn't work, she would head home and try her luck tomorrow.

She turned into an alley behind an old warehouse and crawled out of the rain into a nook behind a loose board in the wall. She had found it a few months ago, by accident, while tracking a missing pet iguana for a merchant's youngest daughter. The merchant—the warehouse owner—probably didn't know about this concealed entrance. He had stacked crates from floor to ceiling there, with no passage into the bowels of the warehouse, but she didn't care. She just needed to get into a small dry space for a bit, out of the relentless rain, so she could check her recalcitrant magic one last time. She couldn't even stand up to her full height in the tiny space; it only allowed her to sit with her knees bent.

It was dim in the nook; light only trickled in through a gap between the boards. Enough light for her needs, she thought absently. She wiped her face, giggled at the futility of the gesture—her sleeve was as wet as the rest of her—and fished the dagger out of her bag.

As soon as her fingers closed around the hilt, the magic pulled, strong and crystal clear. She peeked through the gap to orient herself. The magic arrowed towards the river port. Why hadn't it done that before? Suddenly, she knew. Her target was probably on a boat, and as long as the boat was in motion, its movement confused her finding powers. The boat had probably just docked and thus stopped moving. And her magic responded as it always did. Drat! She should've known.

Altenay dropped the dagger back inside her satchel and eyed the rain outside with distaste. She didn't want to leave her cozy and dry refuge. Hurried footsteps rushed past her hiding place, splashing in the growing puddles. She cocked her head to see the face through her peeking hole and recoiled. The same bearded man she thought might be spying on her stopped in the blind end of the alley and whirled around, his eyes sweeping the muddy ground and the weathered walls of the warehouses. Altenay sat very still, afraid to breathe. He had been following her after all. Her intuition was correct, but why? What would he do if he did find her? She shivered.

Fortunately, he couldn't see her cranny behind the loose board—she had lowered it back in place to cut out the rain. He swore viciously and jogged back to the mouth of the alley. She couldn't see that far without moving the board, and she wasn't foolish enough to do that, but she could hear him swearing for a while longer before his obscenities stopped reaching her ears.

She stayed in her hidey-hole for several more minutes before she found the courage to crawl out. Nameless dread gripped her. The bearded man planned something nasty, she could sense it, but for now, he was nowhere in sight. Must be grateful for small favors, she thought wryly. Perhaps he had decided she was not worth his trouble. Still wary, she made her way to the port, but she didn't see him again.

With her hand inside the satchel, touching the dagger, her magic guided her, but navigating the convoluted maze of the port, crowded with sailors and laborers, delivery wagons and pedestrian vendors, took time. The hubbub had almost deafened her by the time her magic stopped tugging sideways. Instead it zoomed in on a large river barge. A young sailor on the pier was tying a mooring rope. A tall Bessar man with a mane of graying hair, wet and plastered to his head from the rain, bellowed orders to another sailor, as they secured the sails. Altenay's magic latched on the older skipper. She had found her target. This man had definitely handled the dagger in the past.

CAPTAIN BULAT

The skipper noticed her, hopped off his barge, and ambled towards her. An old ragged scar crossed his forehead under the hair. "What are you gawking at, girl?" He towered over her.

"I'm looking for..." She hesitated before pulling the dagger out of her satchel, so he could see it. "...Captain Bulat. I'm a Finder. I was hired to find you."

"No one by that name here," he said briskly. He glanced at the dagger with interest but no recognition. "Are you going to stab me with this? You should remove the sheath first."

"Goodness, no! I'm going to tell you you're him. You're Bulat. My magic is never wrong. My client gave me this dagger, your dagger, and it led me directly to you."

"A dagger? Are you sure?" He frowned. "What was the name again?"

"Captain Bulat," she repeated. He was behaving strangely, staring at her, as if hoping for a miracle. Everything about this case was strange, but her magic still spun around him. She didn't make a mistake, even though he looked baffled.

"Maybe," he said at last. "I don't remember. Why are you looking for this fellow Bulat?"

It was Altenay's turn to stare. "Maybe? He...you were a hero in the last war. You don't remember? The Council wants to erect a statue in your honor."

He barked a surprised laugh. "A statue? I don't think so. I'm no hero. Look, I don't remember what happened during the war. Soon after it ended, Sart, the old skipper of this barge, found me naked and senseless in one of the alleys here, in the city, my head bashed in and my clothes stolen. He took me in. When I came to, I didn't remember anything that happened before. I still don't. It was years ago and it doesn't bother me anymore. I have a new life. As I didn't remember my name at the time, Sart gave me a new one. I go by Master Madan these days, and that's my barge." With obvious pride, he nodded back at his vessel. "Calico Cat."

"You don't remember? But what should I tell my client?" Altenay asked helplessly.

"I don't know." He shrugged. "Tell him that you talked to me. My story is no secret. Everyone knows it along the river, everywhere the Cat docks." He clapped her on the shoulder. "I should get back to work, lass. Good day." He stomped back to his barge, his amused rumbling trailing after him. "A statue, huh."

Altenay sighed and headed for home. She would have to inform the councilor of her finding and its unexpected twist. She had accepted his money after all but she hoped nothing bad would happen to Captain Bulat. Or rather to Master Madan, the skipper of the Calico Cat.

The next day, the cold rain still fell, shrouding the entire city. Councilor Shamer's mansion on the Hill rose defiantly out of the rain, its red marble columns like screams of color, intimidating anyone who dared to approach. The butler opening the front door to Altenay's knock looked down his long nose at her, huddling in her old cloak under the portico.

"Back door," he said haughtily and started closing the door.

"I have a personal message for Councilor Shamer," Altenay said hurriedly. "He said I should bring it to him personally. I'm a Finder. He asked me to find someone."

"Back door." He jerked his head to the right and slammed the door shut.

It figured with the rest of this odd job, Altenay thought sullenly, trudging around the imposing building to its back door. Unlike the ostentatious front with its open view of a wide avenue, the back door was narrow and unadorned, as if hidden shamefully behind a tall dense hedge of junipers in a deserted corner of the grounds.

A servant who met her at the back door behaved almost as snootily as the butler, although he did let her in, grudgingly, and led her to a small antechamber to await the councilor's pleasure. At least she was out of the rain for now.

She settled on a hard bench, leaned on the wall behind her, and prepared to wait. She didn't expect to see anyone for a long time, certainly not the bearded man who had followed her yesterday. Altenay tensed involuntary and jumped up. Was the man supposed to be here? Today, he wore some nondescript clothing, not the Council livery, and he radiated menace. She shrank from him. Should she run back outside?

"You have a message for Councilor Shamer?" he said coldly. "You're the Finder. Give me the message and you can go. I'll deliver it to my master."

Altenay swallowed uneasily. She didn't think she should be talking to this man. "The councilor said that I'm to deliver any messages to him personally. I can't disobey his instructions and give my message to anyone else."

"Did you find him, damn it? Did you find Bulat?" He stepped closer to her.

She inched away, her throat dry from the inexplicable loathing in his eyes. Mutely, she shook her head. "Please," she whispered. "I need to talk to the councilor."

"No, you don't. Get out!" he commanded, crowding her towards the back door.

Didn't the servant who had let her in inform the councilor about her? Should she tell this creepy fellow what she found? Her instincts warned her to keep mum. Perhaps she could talk to the councilor some other time.

The man's iron grip held her shoulder with

bruising strength, propelling her towards the back door. Altenay's heart sped up. Why was he pushing her out with such force? She wasn't resisting. Should she yell for help? Frantically, she looked around, but the narrow corridor was empty.

She was practically at the door when her hand closed over the dagger in her satchel. Should she give it back now? A surge of her magic took her by surprise. It pointed straight at her tormentor. Why was he following her outside? What was her magic telling her? Was this man the real Captain Bulat, and not the friendly amnesiac skipper of the Calico Cat?

Disoriented, she stumbled over the threshold, her finger jerked on the safety catch of the dagger, and it came free of the sheath in her grip. She landed hard on her butt on the wet gravel of the path. Only her fall allowed her to see the flash of his knife, as he, unable to abort his own momentum, slashed the air where her neck had been a moment ago. He swore and lifted the knife again, now aiming correctly at her, still sitting stupidly on the ground.

Altenay didn't even have time to think. Numb with terror, she felt like a puppet, with someone else pulling her strings. Her hand holding the dagger shot up to block the lethal trajectory of his knife. Simultaneously, she shifted on the hard ground, trying to get away from him, and her assailant tripped on her outstretched leg. He tottered for a moment, shouted something unintelligible, and fell, embedding himself on her dagger. He grunted, his knife-holding hand flopped aimlessly, his eyes rolled back, and his dead weight knocked her down. She screamed just as her head struck a rock at the side of the path. Then everything went black.

When she came to, she was in a large and opulent room, lying on a sofa under a mirror in a carved gilded frame. She ached all over. Her head throbbed. A big fat woman in servant's clothing stood at the window with her back to the room. Altenay made a sound, and the woman turned.

"You're awake, dear," she said, her eyes kind but watchful. "About time. Milord wants to talk to you. Can you talk to him now?"

Altenay's eyes skimmed around the room, registering the painted ceiling, the heavy portiere embroidered with gold, and the expensive rosewood furniture with the pearly mosaic inlays.

"What happened?" she asked hoarsely and coughed to clear her throat. She remembered going to see the councilor to tell him about the skipper. After that, her memory became hazy. "Could I have some water, please?"

"Of course." The woman poured water from a crystal decanter and brought the glass to Altenay. "That's what we all want to know," she said. "What happened? Can you sit, dear?"

Altenay swung her feet down, but she moved too fast. She squeezed her eyes shut against the vertigo.

"Slowly, dear. No rush." The woman's gentle hand steadied her.

After a few moments, the dizziness subsided, and Altenay was able to open her eyes and sip the water. Her hands holding the glass shook, but her memory trickled back. The dreadful man. The knife. She gasped and looked down at herself, dressed only in her tunic and trousers. No bloody wounds.

"Where is my cloak? And my satchel?"

"The cloak was all bloody. I soaked it in cold water to get the blood out. Your satchel is over there." The woman nodded at the side table beside the sofa."

"What happened to that man? He attacked me. Why did he attack me?" Panic, mixed with nausea, clawed at Altenay's insides.

"I don't know. You should talk to the milord."

"But I..." Tears welled in her eyes. "Did I kill that man, his servant?"

"He was no servant in this house," the woman said firmly. "I've never seen him before. The milord is investigating now, asking who let the stranger in, but I don't think you're in any danger. The milord is a fair master, and that bounder obviously attacked you first. I'll tell the milord you're awake." She vanished behind a door.

Altenay leaned on the sofa's back and closed her eyes. She couldn't escape anyway. She doubted she could walk yet. Her whole body felt as boneless as a sack of jelly, and her head swam. She lifted her hand to touch the throbbing spot on her head and hissed, as her fingers encountered a large painful lump at the back of her head, beneath the hair. "Where is my tubeteika?" she mumbled. "It was my favorite." She wanted to cry but swallowed the constriction in her throat. What was the point? She would probably lose much more than her tubeteika soon. She shouldn't have taken this damn job.

Councilor Shamer strode into the room a few minutes later, his bodyguards flanking him. "Mistress Finder." He pulled a chair towards the sofa and sat down, his face grim. "What happened? Why did my servants find you at the back door, unconscious, with a man who had obviously assaulted you with his knife on top of you? Dead. By the dagger I gave you."

"I came to see you," Altenay said wearily. She didn't lift her head from the back of the sofa. It was soft and comfortable. She didn't want to move. "I don't know why he attacked me. He demanded I tell him my message, but you said that any messages should be delivered to you personally, so I didn't. Then he pushed me out the door and pulled his knife on me." She eyed the councilor with resentment. "He followed me yesterday too, while I searched for Captain Bulat.

CAPTAIN BULAT

Why did you set him to spy on me?"

"I didn't. Nobody spied on you. Certainly not that man. He doesn't work for me. He is, or rather he was, a courier for the City Council." He leaned forward. "Did you find Bulat?"

"I don't know what I found," Altenay said. "I thought I did, but when I touched the dagger today, when that man jumped me, my magic pointed at him too. I don't know why. He is not Captain Bulat, is he?"

"No." Shamer frowned in puzzlement. "You magic pointed towards this man?"

"Maybe he wears something that belonged to Captain Bulat, like the dagger? Where is the dagger?"

"I have it." He beckoned one of his bodyguards, whispered something in his ear, and the man left the room.

"The sheath is probably still in my satchel. You should take it too," Altenay said. "Let me tell you what I found yesterday." She proceeded to tell him the skipper's story.

The councilor listened without interruption. "Lost his memory for twenty-five years?" he said skeptically, when she finished.

"I don't know, Milord, but he sounded convincing. I believed him. He said people know his story all along the river, in every port. You could check."

"Why did you talk to him? I told you not to."

Altenay shrugged and lied: "My magic behaved strangely. I had to be sure."

"Everything about this case is strange," he said. He didn't seem angry.

"Yes, Milord."

The bodyguard returned, bringing the dagger. Briefly he consulted with his employer.

"Take the dagger, Finder," said the councilor, "and see where your magic points right now."

Altenay obeyed, and the bodyguard tensed visibly.

She grinned. Did he think her an assassin? She concentrated, wincing at the ache in her head, and the magic leaped readily to her service, as it always did, pointing straight at the guard. Altenay opened her mouth in surprise. Her magic had never been so erratic before. "At him!"

The guard opened his palm, revealing a tarnished silver medallion on a chain.

"Probably at the medallion," said the councilor dryly. "Try again."

Altenay did. "Yes, you're right. Did the medallion belong to Captain Bulat?"

"Yes. Bulat never took it off, but for some reason, your attacker wore it today." He stood up abruptly. "Seems to corroborate your story. Come, Finder. I'll take you home in my carriage. After all, you've been injured in my service. But before that, we'll make a detour to the port. I want to see that skipper. You think he is still in port?" He eyed her with an odd, almost hopeful expression.

"I think so," Altenay said slowly. "He only docked yesterday. The cargo barges usually stay in port for two days, to unload and load again. He should be loading today." Then a doubt surfaced. "It is still today? How long have I been unconscious?"

"Not long. This morning, there was no one at the back door."

"What time is it now?"

"A little after noon."

"Thank you," Altenay murmured. No, not long. Probably a few minutes. Still unsteady on her feet, she swayed, and one of the bodyguards caught her when she started to topple. He waited until she felt better, his grip on her elbows oddly reassuring.

"He could carry you," the councilor said.

"No, no, I'm fine. I can walk. I think. Let me try." She wriggled out of her supporter's hands and took a few wobbly steps. To her relief, she was right. She could walk.

The carriage was roomy, its crimson plushy seats almost as comfortable as the sofa. Altenay leaned back and sighed in satisfaction. She could live in this carriage with its embroidered curtains and soft velvet squabs.

The councilor chuckled and settled across from her. Taking a fur rug from the seat beside him, he draped it over her knees. She pulled it up and snuggled into it. It was big enough to cover all of her, and she was chilly without her cloak. The bodyguards stayed outside. The carriage started rolling.

"Where is your tubeteika?" the councilor asked abruptly.

"I don't know. I lost it somewhere in the scuffle. I had it on when I came in."

"If my servants find it, I'll send it back to you, together with your cloak," he promised.

"Thank you, Milord. I thought you didn't like my tubeteika."

He snorted. "You probably have questions."

"I do, but the most pressing one is: what is going to happen to me after I killed that man?"

"Nothing. I suggest you forget the entire episode. He attacked you, you defended yourself. I only regret that it happened in my house."

"Technically it happened outside, on your doorstep," Altenay said. By now, she felt easy enough with him to attempt a joke. The councilor didn't seem as scary as before. Maybe her fracas with the bearded man put everything into the right perspective.

"Quite...technically." He lapsed into brooding. "You know, I hated Bulat for twenty-five years. Before that, he was my best friend. And now, I'm starting to realize that my hatred might've been misdirected. What a mess."

"What happened?"

He stared at her but she didn't think he saw her. He was reliving his past when he started speaking again. "We were friends during the war, Bulat and I. The night he disappeared, we played cards. I lost and didn't have the money to pay him. I gave him my coat instead. It had diamond buttons. I forgot that I had some sensitive letters in the coat's pocket. When I sobered up and remembered a few hours later, I went to retrieve the letters, but he was gone, and so was my coat. Then the blackmail demands started and they went on for twenty-five years. I thought it was him, but if he was robbed and left for dead that same night, then it was someone else. Probably someone connected with that courier you so inconveniently killed. Never mind. I'll find his master. I should've started the investigation much sooner. So many years wasted."

"I'm sorry, Milord."

He didn't acknowledge her pity and didn't say anything else all the way to the river port. When they halted in front of the pier where the Calico Cat bobbed on her mooring, the councilor left her in the carriage. Altenay watched him talk to the skipper although she couldn't hear a word. In the end, the men shook hands and smiled at each other. Then they hugged. Both looked suffused with the same inner fire. It still smoldered when the councilor clambered back into the carriage.

"It seems your reputation was deserved, Finder," he said with a fleeting grin. "You did find my hero for me. Master Madan, the skipper of the Calico Cat—I'd never have guessed."

"So he's your Captain Bulat?"

"Yes, he is."

"Is he still a hero if he doesn't remember?"

"Yes," the councilor said. "The others remember

for him." He eyed her with a speculative gleam in his sharp eyes. "Perhaps you could find my blackmailer too?"

"Perhaps," Altenay said. "But not today, and judging by the recent events, I'd need a bodyguard of my own for such a search. I don't want to fight off another crazed killer. I'm no hero myself. I'm a Finder who just got lucky."

"Searching and finding unknown things could be quite a heroic occupation…sometimes."

"Sometimes." She allowed herself a small smile. "Most of the times it is just a job."

"Of course, Finder," he said.

The End

Olga Godim is a fantasy writer and journalist from Vancouver, Canada. Her short stories have been published in multiple internet and print magazines. Her fantasy novels ALMOST ADEPT and EAGLE EN GARDE were released by Champagne/Burst in 2014. In 2015, EAGLE EN GARDE won EPIC eBook Award in the Fantasy category. Aside from writing fantasy, Olga writes articles for a local Vancouver newspaper, designs book covers, and collects toy monkeys. There are over 300 monkeys in her collection. You could find her online at her site: www.olgagodim.wordpress.com

The Witch Bottle
By Sean McLachlan

"You must piss in it, sir," Malcolm said as he handed the bottle to his master.

Henry Raban, Esquire, took a final puff of Virginia tobacco and set his clay pipe on the mantelpiece. He gave his servant a doubtful look as he took the bottle offered to him.

It was half again the length of his hand and made of heavy crockery. The neck had the design of a face stamped into the clay—a bearded man with crazed hair sticking out in all directions, as if he had been riding his horse at a fast gait all day. The eyes wide and staring. Henry suppressed a shudder as he turned to Malcolm.

"Is this absolutely necessary?" he asked.

Malcolm nodded, "It is, sir, if you want to trap the filthy witch who torments you. Such evil women are—"

"I'll remind you that you are speaking of my wife!" Henry snapped.

Malcolm bowed and mumbled an apology. Henry grunted and looked back at the bottle in his hand.

"But witch she is, and torment me she does. If you say that pissing in this thing will trap her, then I must make haste to the privy. That ale you served with the venison has worked its way through me."

When Henry returned to his sitting room, careful not to spill the sloshing contents of the bottle, he found Malcolm busy at his desk—Henry's desk. The gentleman resisted the urge to upbraid his servant.

That man thinks himself above his station, Henry

THE WITCH BOTTLE

mused, *but he is essential to me. I only wish he weren't so cognizant of the fact.*

"What are you doing now?" Henry asked.

"Other items to trap the witch," Malcolm said, indicating the pile of odds and ends littering the desk. "Twelve iron nails, eight brass pins, and a twist to the heart."

Malcolm held up a small patch of leather cut in the shape of a heart. A bent iron nail was stuck through the middle.

"Ah, that should catch her!" Henry said. "She loves me still, I'll wager ten guineas."

"Most assuredly. We need some more items, sir. Kindly give me the bottle. My, I fear I did indeed serve you too much ale for supper."

Malcolm turned to the window and poured out some of the yellow fluid onto the rose bushes. He then dropped the nails, pins, and leather heart into the bottle.

"Now kindly sit down, sir, and I will cut your fingernails."

Henry shook his head and sat down. Although Malcolm had explained the process after the curse had started, Henry still didn't like the idea. His wife's witchery was all too real, but surely participating in such a thing as the creation of a witch bottle would be considered almost as ungodly. He had his reputation to consider.

Malcolm set to work trimming Henry's nails with a tiny pair of shears, dropping each cutting one by one into the bottle. After that he unbuttoned Henry's shirt without so much as a by-your-leave and plucked the fluff from his navel. This went into the bottle too. Malcolm looked inside, gave a satisfied nod, and stoppered the bottle, sealing it with wax from a dripping candle that sat lit on the desk despite the warm spring sunshine pouring in from the open

HERO LOST: MYSTERIES OF DEATH AND LIFE

window.

* * *

Catherine Raban stood at the window of the little cottage that was once again her home. She looked east, towards her husband's fine twelve-room estate that had once been hers, though it stood a few leagues away over a stream and past two villages.

But magic flies faster than the swiftest steed.

"It is still mine," she said to the empty room.

She had been the belle of the village since she was thirteen. All the young swains wanted her, all the wealthy old men vied to have her as their house maid. But her mother had been wise. Oh, her mother! She had learned so much from her—the Craft, the secrets of plants and stars, and the subtler craft that all women have, not only those who have inherited the Gift. Yes, her mother had kept her close, refusing munificent offers for her employ, chasing off the young bucks and laying a curse on those who proved too insistent. Mother and daughter knew Henry Raban's first wife hadn't long to live and that he looked at Catherine with eyes as covetous as any man's.

Shortly after Catherine turned sixteen, Henry Raban's wife met her Maker. No Craft had been required. Mother insisted on that. God called the woman, and no wagging tongue could say they had had a hand in it.

After an unsuitably short period of mourning, Henry came to Catherine's mother asking for the girl's hand in marriage. From this one-room cottage, Catherine moved into a brick house with a maid, a cook, and a manservant. A fine coach took her on rides around Henry's ample lands. *Her* lands.

Now all that was gone, and her mother gone, too, poor woman, taken by God or the Devil or neither, as some in the coven whispered. That was the most blasphemous truth the Craft could utter—that there

THE WITCH BOTTLE

was no Heaven or Hell, only the laws of nature, action and reaction, sympathy and antipathy. All in one, each thing isolate, each thing temporary. All endures.

She had not sat out the blush of her youth, not resisted the charms of the young men who came calling, not given her maidenhead to a portly, balding oaf only to lose the wealth her mother never had.

She picked up the doll, dressed in a coat woven from her husband's own hair, which she had meticulously collected from his comb over the course of three long years. Her finger rested on the end of a pin stuck in the doll's stomach. She grasped it. She twisted.

* * *

"My God, oh, but it hurts!" Henry shouted, clutching his ample belly.

"She's using her witchery again," Malcolm said, leaping up and grabbing some coal from the scuttle next to the hearth. "Now is the time to act."

"Make haste! It feels as if a rapier is skewering my insides."

Malcolm stoked the fire as Henry moaned in his easy chair. Once the flames burned high and bright, Malcolm grabbed the witch bottle. Henry looked hopefully at his servant as Malcolm brandished the bottle over the fire, then started passing it through the flames.

"Now your little witch will feel the fire as if it were scorching her own flesh."

"The pain is easing," Henry said.

"Her hold on you is loosening."

* * *

In the cottage, Catherine wailed as she gripped the windowsill with white knuckles. Sweat slicked her body as her face grew as red as sunset. She gritted her teeth, knotted her brow, and straightened her spine.

* * *

HERO LOST: MYSTERIES OF DEATH AND LIFE

The witch bottle shattered. Fragments of crockery clattered against the slate of the hearth as Henry's piss splashed onto Malcolm's trousers.

"Blast!" the servant cried.

"Is she beaten?" Henry asked hopefully.

"No," Malcolm grumbled.

"But I feel no pain."

"She is hurt. That is why she is not tormenting you. But make no mistake; she will recover her powers and return."

Malcolm stalked toward the door.

"Don't leave me!" Henry wailed.

"I'm merely changing my trousers, you booby," the servant called back over his shoulder as he walked out.

Henry scowled at the door and then gave the shattered bottle in the hearth a terrified look.

* * *

Catherine lay in her bed, breathing deeply and trying not to remember the pain. *Malcolm. It had to have been him.* From the moment he'd set foot in Henry's home, she'd been wary of the fellow. Malcolm had come from nobody-knew-where, with references Henry never checked and Catherine never believed. He listened too carefully, stared too long, and knew too much to be a manservant. Even more suspicious, he proved immune to her charms. Not that she'd consent to tumble with a man now beneath her station, but he at least should melt at her smile like other men did.

Malcolm soon had her husband under his thumb. Her authority usurped in every room but the bedroom, the only room in the mansion she hated, she watched with fury as Henry increased Malcolm's wages and bought him a new set of clothes and a pair of shoes with silver buckles.

Mother hadn't raised her to be the kind of woman

THE WITCH BOTTLE

to sit idly by. Soon Malcolm came down with the chills. Warts covered his face, and from his nose ran green pus. But Malcolm was a wily one and looked under his straw tick to find the rancid piece of sheep's kidney wrapped in a frog's skin.

Malcolm denounced her to the magistrate. The constabulary searched her things and found more evidence of the Craft. To avoid a scandal, Henry had the whole thing hushed up. The magistrate and constables pocketed the money, but insisted that Catherine leave the village. Henry bedded her one last time and sent her on her way.

* * *

"We have to go through this entire demeaning process again?" Henry grumbled.

"Yes, sir," Malcolm said, now wearing his Sunday best while the maid sat with a washtub in the backyard scrubbing his work clothes. "As fortune would have it, I have another witch bottle same as the last. We must fill it again with pins, your water, your nails—"

"My fingernails are cut to the quick!"

"Your toenails, then. This time we'll catch her, I promise you."

"She resisted the fire."

"She's a strong one, to be sure. We must be cleverer than she. There are other ways to catch a witch than fire."

"Such as?"

"You shall see, sir, you shall see."

* * *

Catherine sat at her mother's table, mixing herbs with a mortar and pestle. Every now and then she'd reach over and give the pin in her husband's effigy a twist.

"Let's see, rosebuds, lavender, and ginger should get him pining for me, orange flowers to remember to be loyal in marriage, and a dash of St. John's Wort will help with forgetfulness, so he'll let this curse be bygones. In the meantime, though, the selfish poltroon needs a bit more of *this*."

With that, she gave the pin another twist.

A knock at the door made her look up. She stuffed the effigy of her husband into the pocket of her smock and threw a cheesecloth over her preparations. Wiping her hands, she went to the door.

A boy she recognized from her husband's estate stood outside. He took a step back as she opened the door, stared at her slack-jawed for a moment, and held out a letter.

"Don't tremble so. I'll not hurt you," Catherine said as she took the note from his hand.

She opened it.

Dearest Catherine,

I cannot live another moment without you. I know you feel the same. All is forgiven. Let our love bloom again this spring after the winter of our discontent.

Love always, your husband and master,

Henry

Catherine gave a bitter laugh, tore up the letter, and told the boy, who was obviously waiting for a reply while resisting the urge to run, "Tell that fool that if he wants me back, he has to give me a security. In writing. I'll not be welcomed back only to be cast aside again."

The boy nodded and ran off.

* * *

"Oh, it's worse than ever before!" Henry wailed.

"We must bleed you, sir," Malcolm said.

"Bleed me?"

"To remove the foul humours her curse has put into your blood."

"I will send a boy to get the surgeon."

"No, sir! He would be sure to see that you are under a curse. Think of the scandal!"

THE WITCH BOTTLE

Henry clutched his belly again, face scrunched in pain.

"Oooooh, what do I care for scandal? This pain must stop."

"It will be only a prick of the finger, sir, no need for the surgeon."

"Very well, but make haste!"

Malcolm fetched a pin and a small glass vial. He pricked Henry's finger, which elicited barely a jerk from the man since he was so overwhelmed with the pain in his stomach, and squeezed the tip of his finger so that several drops fell into the bottle. Malcolm then put a cork in the bottle and turned to walk away.

"What are you doing?" Henry asked.

"The most powerful ingredient in a witches' curses is a man's blood, as surely you have heard it said. I must bury this blood so that Catherine does not find it and use it against you."

As Malcolm left the room, Henry bent over in pain.

"Malcolm! Malcolm!" he grunted through clenched teeth. "The foul humours have not left my body! It hurts as much as ever!"

* * *

Malcolm ignored his master's pleas and went to his own room. Once there, he unstopped the bottle of blood and mixed it with a bottle of ink, one of several ink bottles with different labels hidden under his bed. He took the bottle of mixed blood and ink, and strode back to Henry's drawing room.

He found his master sprawled across his easy chair in a cold sweat, holding a document.

"You were wise to write that up ahead of time in case of such an eventuality," Malcolm said. "Assigning your wife rights to half your estate, even in case of divorce, will surely get her back."

"It pains me to do this, but I must have her back. She loves me still. Oh, how my mistrust of her must have struck pain in her tender heart!"

Malcolm rolled his eyes, and then looked nervously at his master. No, the fool hadn't seen. He upbraided himself for his uncharacteristic slip of showing his true feelings, but how much whining could one be expected to take?

* * *

Catherine sat knitting by the window. She hadn't twisted the pin for some time now, hoping her forbearance would make her husband more pliable.

Husband, Catherine snorted. *Husband only for money.* There were others far more deserving of her maidenhead and her hand in marriage. Like Jonathon, who at age twelve had bloodied the nose of a bully two years his elder and a hand span taller for saying that Catherine's mother rode a broomstick on full moons. Or Albert, ah sweet Albert! Her first kiss at thirteen, and not a word her mother could say that would make her regret it. A handsome lad was he, now gone a sailor and no doubt making the lasses swoon in the West Indies. She'll never see those fine features again. If she had married him, he would have never left for the sea...

A knock at the door brought her out of the past and into the present. She opened it to find the boy was back, with a new letter in his hand. As she took it, he ran off.

She opened it and read,

My darling, all is forgiven. Please come back to me. I know my mistrust has disappointed you, but it cannot have dampened the love you have always shown me.

Catherine laughed out loud.

Below is a legal document guaranteeing you half my lands, monies, and property portable and immoveable. Plus, I will dismiss Malcolm, who I know you have always disliked.

Catherine raised an eyebrow.

THE WITCH BOTTLE

Anything to make you happy.

Catherine continued reading and found that the document did, indeed, say all Henry claimed it said. It was signed with his own hand, with the cook, not Malcolm, as witness.

Catherine clapped her hands with joy. She was reinstated to her rightful place, and that dastard Malcolm was out on his ear! She wondered about the judge and the constables. What would they say if she reappeared at the estate? Henry must have bought them off. A pretty penny was gone from the family coffers, to be sure, but no matter. A bit of Craft would increase Henry's harvest as it had last year, and the expense would soon be recouped. She grabbed her shawl and bonnet, and hurried out the door.

* * *

"She torments me no longer," Henry said as he watched Malcolm digging a hole in front of the threshold.

"Her heart has turned towards you, sir," Malcolm replied without looking up from his work.

"So is the witch bottle still necessary?" Henry asked.

"Surely, sir. As I said, burying the bottle upside down and having her pass over it will tie her to you and this property forever. She will never leave you."

"Ah, but she loves me! There is no need for enchantment."

"But sir, women are a fickle lot, witches or otherwise. It's best to be sure."

"Yes, Malcolm, I suppose you're correct. You always know what's best."

Once the hole was deep enough, Malcolm placed the witch bottle in it upside down and covered it with dirt. He smoothed it over and replaced the gravel of the front walk. It looked as if it had never been disturbed.

HERO LOST: MYSTERIES OF DEATH AND LIFE

"That is certainly good work," Henry said as he stepped out of door. Malcolm restrained him.

"Not yet, sir! The witch must be the first to pass over the bottle for the magic to take effect. That is why I gave the rest of the servants the afternoon off. Sit in the front room, visible through the window, while I secrete myself in the back. She will be here soon, and you will have your heart's desire."

"That I will," Henry rubbed his hands with glee. "In fact it might be best if you stayed at the inn tonight. It will be a noisy time here, and you shan't get any sleep. Here's a guinea for your trouble. By the time you return in the morning, there will be no more talk of your leaving. I will have her well in hand."

Malcolm bowed and smiled.

"That she will, sir, that she will."

Henry sat as he had been told in the front room, visible from the road. He didn't have long to wait. Soon a familiar figure came strolling along the lane, a few stray blond tresses flowing out of her bonnet to catch the sunlight like gold. Henry leapt up out of his chair and almost forgot Malcolm's injunction to stay put. He controlled himself, fidgeting as Catherine turned off the lane and walked up the path to the house.

Henry trembled a little and bit his lower lip.

Ah, but she is a beauty! Henry thought. *Every man in the shire was green with envy when she married me. But why does she scowl so? Shouldn't she be happy? The poor girl is still cross with me. Who could blame her after the way I treated her? That will soon be smoothed over. With Malcolm's spell, and my own prowess in bed, she'll be as meek as a lamb by sunrise.*

His heart grew light as Catherine approached and looked at him. A smile replaced her frown.

"My love," she said, extending her arms as she walked up to the door.

THE WITCH BOTTLE

"Welcome home," Henry said and stepped across the threshold.

Arms wide to embrace each other, they came together over the spot where the witch bottle lay buried. And disappeared.

* * *

Malcolm smiled as he dug through the dirt with his hands. He felt smooth ceramic beneath the soil and soon uncovered the bottle. He picked it up and found it warm to the touch.

"Having a hot time in there, are you?" he chuckled.

He walked back into the house and packed the witch bottle into a small crate padded with straw. He'd bury it in the woods come nightfall. Nobody would ever find it. After he tucked the crate under his bed, he reached into his coat and withdrew two documents. The first was the document he'd tricked Henry into signing. While Henry thought he was signing a legal document to give his wife half the estate, in fact, he was signing a document giving Malcolm the entire estate, with generous remunerations to the other servants to keep them silent. The two documents had been written one over the other with two different types of ink—one that disappears immediately and then reappears over time, and the other that fades within a day and a night, never to be seen again.

The second document was the one that was now visible on the page. A third type of ink had been used to sign it, the ink tainted with Henry's own blood. To sign a document in blood made one a witch. And a witch could be captured in a witch bottle.

Feeling very pleased with himself, Malcolm tucked the documents back into his coat. He put on his coat and prepared to take a stroll around the property. *His* property.

A series of high-pitched squeaks came from his side pocket as a blob of darkness poked out of it. It looked like a moving inkblot with arms and legs that scrabbled with tiny claws up the side of his coat.

"We've done well, my friend, we've done well," Malcolm said, tucking the demon back in his pocket.

The End

Sean McLachlan is the author of numerous novels, including three series: Toxic World (post-apocalyptic science fiction), House Divided (Civil War horror), and the Trench Raiders action series set in World War One. You can find out more about him here:

Blog: www.midlistwriter.blogspot.com

Facebook: www.facebook.com/pages/Sean-McLachlan/287407921290111

Newsletter: http://eepurl.com/bJfiDn

The Art of Remaining Bitter
By Yvonne Ventresca

Sylvia sat at the kitchen table, kicking the legs of her older sister's empty chair. She had run out of time at school yesterday, so she woke early Saturday to finish her math lesson. Word problems were the worst, but Sylvia was determined to do as well as her sister. Caralea had always earned high marks when she was in sixth grade. Resolute, she focused on the first question.

Six ducklings traveled 117 miles in 3 hours. What's the average rate they flew?

Sylvia stared out the apartment window, which overlooked the vast forest to the east of the big gate. She tried to imagine what existed 117 miles away, but pine trees extended as far as she could see.

How far could she run in three hours if she left the safety of their community for the forest and didn't stop? She had a babysitter, Kona, back when her parents took Caralea to endless doctor visits. While they made art projects to pass the time, Kona used to tell stories, like the one about a secret path outside the gate. When you turned twelve and left for your Bliss procedure, you could take the trail to escape having it done. When Sylvia asked about returning home, Kona acted mysterious. It was tricky, she explained, but not impossible. "When you're older I'll tell you more," Kona promised.

Sylvia asked Mom, Dad, and Caralea about the path, but none of them knew, and they questioned why anyone would want to avoid Bliss anyway. Then Kona stopped coming, and Sylvia had mostly forgotten about what the babysitter said and her promise to explain.

But as Sylvia's birthday approached and her time for Bliss neared, she couldn't help but wonder. She'd grilled her best friend about the entire procedure after Ashley turned twelve a few weeks ago. But Ashley hadn't seen any secret path.

Sylvia was still staring out at the forest when Dad joined her in the kitchen to make his daily cup of coffee. "Busy day," he said. "There's a push to increase harvesting for the Festival. We can't run out of food on the big day." The Festival of Joy was the one day of the year when food seemed plentiful. It was a happy celebration with community decorations and a giant parade. "Are you ready to help? I really need you and Caralea today."

Dad helped manage the farm, and on Saturdays he often brought the girls with him. They were allowed to pick fruit and vegetables for testing. "Random sampling" he called it. Saturday was Sylvia's favorite day of the week.

"Yes!" she said.

"Great. We'll leave after Mom and Caralea get home from the fabric store."

Sylvia didn't want to wait. But she tucked her long hair behind her ears and refocused on her homework. One problem down. Nine more to go.

Finally, Caralea and Mom returned with bags of fabric her mother would use to create gowns for the parade. Their loud, cheerful voices overwhelmed the tiny apartment. Caralea's laughter was like glitter shimmering through the air. Glitter annoyed Sylvia.

"We should leave for the farm," Dad said. "There's lots to be done."

They often strolled there leisurely on Saturdays,

but today they rode bikes to arrive quickly. Dad led the way, followed by Caralea, then Sylvia. Other than her pale skin, there were no signs that Caralea had been ill. She certainly pedaled fast enough.

"It's a beautiful day," Caralea said over her shoulder.

Sylvia ignored her. Every day was beautiful to her sister. She stood as she pushed on the pedals, picking up speed until she passed Caralea with a gleeful smile. Caralea, unperturbed, gave her a friendly wave and continued to ride behind her.

Excitement buzzed through Sylvia as they approached the farm. The glass building towered forty stories high, with floor after floor of produce extending up into the sky. Most floors appeared green from a distance, but if she looked closely, she could make out the orange carrot level above the red of the tomatoes. Art was her favorite subject at school, and she always thought the farm looked like a painting, cheerful and lively.

They would be working among the tubers today, but first Dad let them stop at the berry floor. The girls were allowed to help with a taste test, one strawberry, raspberry, and blueberry each. They agreed that the fruit was ripe and delicious. While Caralea helped Dad enter the details into the harvest database, Sylvia snuck one of the plump blue circles into her pocket for later.

Ashley's mom worked at the farm, too. She was busy checking the nutrient levels when they arrived at the potato section.

Sylvia walked over to her. "Hi, Mrs. Peters. Is Ashley here today?"

Mrs. Peters jumped. "Oh, Sylvia. You startled me. She's home watching her brother."

"Okay. Tell her I said hi."

Sylvia hurried back to receive her instructions for

HERO LOST: MYSTERIES OF DEATH AND LIFE

the afternoon. Dad gave each girl the coordinates of the plants they should take a potato from, along with a labeled tray to put the samples in. It was like a food treasure hunt. Sylvia skipped along, filling her tray from the appropriate section. She was fast, but she was careful, checking the plant coordinates twice before removing any vegetables. She raced back to Dad with her full tray while Caralea was still gathering.

Dad smiled at her with pride. "Maybe you'll work here someday." She grabbed another tray and the next set of coordinates, eager to help. But she didn't have the heart to tell him that she would only want to work with fruit and vegetables as objects for her still life paintings.

Sylvia was deep in the center of the potato plants when the screaming started. She rushed toward the sound with her partially filled tray.

Mrs. Peters stood shrieking between two police officers. When one of them led her away, she let her weight drop until he had to drag her across the floor. Her eyes were wild as her frantic screaming continued.

"I had to report her," Sylvia's father said calmly. "She was stealing."

Sylvia gasped. Crime rarely occurred in their community. She never expected to witness an arrest, especially of someone she knew. Why did Dad have to report her? Their families had been friends her whole life.

But she knew her parents prided themselves on being model citizens because of the special help Caralea had received. Most people underwent a Bliss procedure on their twelfth birthday to remove their negative emotions. Caralea was the first person to be born without any negativity, never needing the procedure at all. Her sister was a miracle of sorts, and when she became ill, the government went through great lengths to save her.

THE ART OF REMAINING BITTER

Mrs. Peters shrieked one last time from across the floor. Then it was silent.

"What will happen to her?" Sylvia asked the remaining police officer. At first, Sylvia thought his badge said "Red," like his hair, but then she realized it was Reed.

"Renewal," Officer Reed said in a tone that discouraged any further questions.

No one knew what went on during Renewal, only that Bliss didn't always work on some people. Renewal didn't take place in the regular hospital, where they had saved Caralea, but in the building behind the Bliss Medical Facility, deep in the woods. After a month, people came back with a blankness to them that Sylvia found disturbing. Poor Ashley. How would she handle a Renewed mother? Would she blame Sylvia's family?

Clutching her stomach at the thought, she ran to the bathroom as her father called her name. Inside the stall, she leaned over, trying to catch her breath. Then she remembered the blueberry in her pocket. She had stolen, too. How would they punish a pre-Bliss eleven-year-old? Not taking any chances, she popped the evidence in her mouth and ate it. It must not have been as ripe as it looked. All she could taste was bitter.

* * *

Dad and Caralea acted fine at dinner, as if nothing terrible had happened. Mom hovered over her as Sylvia scrubbed the plates. Her mother always assigned Caralea the easier chores, like straightening up the linen closet.

"Are you okay?" Mom asked. "I wish we could make you feel better."

"Maybe I don't want to feel better."

"Don't be ridiculous. It will be a relief when you can be more like your sister and not worry as much.

Bliss will be a good thing for you."

Sylvia remembered asking the babysitter why anyone would want to hold on to "bad" emotions. "There are a lot of reasons," Kona had said. "You have an artist's heart. I think eventually you'll understand."

After finishing the dishes, she retreated to her room. Trying to get ahead on her homework, she flipped through the images of famous paintings. *The Starry Night. Water Lilies.* They were supposed to pick one and write about it. Sylvia chose *The Scream.*

* * *

Monday morning, Ashley called to say she'd be late to school, so Sylvia walked alone. Still, she lingered by the main doors, hoping to catch her friend before class. Behind her, Maddox, another kid from her grade, gave her a little shove. "Hurry up," he said.

Startled, she scurried through. He was always nasty. Did he find his negative emotions as useful as she did? He wasn't the kind of person she could ask.

Ashley finally arrived after lunch, but the first chance Sylvia had to talk to her alone was on the walk home. Her friend seemed surprisingly tranquil. "Aren't you worried about your mom?" Sylvia asked.

"It's okay," Ashley said. "She broke the rules. My brother is going through another growth spurt, and with limited food...still, what my mother did was wrong."

"Ashley—"

"It will be fine."

She didn't want to upset her friend. "Okay. If you say so."

"Besides, my brother plans to eat his weight at the Festival."

"That doesn't really solve the problem."

Ashley gave her a look, and she decided to drop it.

"What should we eat first?" Ashley asked. It was a game they played before every Festival, building up

THE ART OF REMAINING BITTER

the anticipation. Ashley swapped her favorite food each year, but Sylvia's was always the same.

"Let me guess," Ashley said. "Chocolate!"

"I...I don't know," Sylvia said slowly, still perturbed by her friend's happy mood. "I don't know if I want chocolate this year. I might choose something different." She couldn't keep the edge out of her voice.

"Maybe after your procedure, you'll have fewer bad feelings and enjoy the Festival more."

"Maybe," Sylvia said. Post-Bliss Ashley was beginning to get on her nerves. "Tell me again what it was like."

"Okay," Ashley said. "My mom walked me to the edge of the woods. Then I followed the trail to the hospital door. A special greeter was there to explain everything. How it's a helpful medical procedure. How it's necessary for our health. Of course, everyone knows that."

Sylvia nodded. They were exposed to the idea of Bliss long before they turned twelve. "Are you sure it wasn't painful?"

"It didn't hurt. I promise."

"It was a small needle or a big one?" Sylvia asked.

"Tiny."

"And then?"

"At first I was afraid, and sad about Grandpa's death, and worried. But when I woke up, I wasn't anymore. The emotions were just gone from me. Like an emptiness, but a good emptiness."

Sylvia frowned.

"What's the matter?" Ashley asked.

"What if...what if I don't want to let my bad feelings go?"

"Don't be silly. There's no reason to hold onto them."

Sylvia watched her non-grieving, somewhat oblivious best friend, and she wasn't so sure.

HERO LOST: MYSTERIES OF DEATH AND LIFE

* * *

Back home, Sylvia gazed out the window of their high-rise building. A new Festival banner fluttered from a nearby balcony. "Festival of Joy" waved in the breeze. Someone in the upper grades must live there. Those students were in charge of making all of the decorations.

She couldn't wait until it was her turn to create banners. She had a lot of ideas. Her most recent one was to write out "Joy" in big, block letters and decorate each one with a different colored food.

But that was years away. She forced herself to focus on her homework and read the tortuous math problems.

If a farm grows 40 strawberries on each plant, and 3200 strawberries are needed for Festival of Joy desserts, how many plants should the farmer grow?

Now there was a question she could understand. She was noting her answer, eighty plants, when Caralea interrupted.

"Look, Sylvia!" She pranced into the kitchen with a badly sketched dress. One thing Caralea couldn't do was draw. "For the parade."

As part of the celebration, giant floats paraded down the streets, each carrying someone special from the community. Caralea was always chosen to ride on a float. Being born with Bliss practically made her a legend. Still, she lacked the glow of other healthy people. Between her pale skin and her dramatic story, everyone knew Caralea.

"What do you think?"

Sylvia thought that no one ever asked if she wanted to ride in the parade. She swallowed the lump in her throat. "Anything Mom sews will be amazing."

Caralea nodded in agreement. "True."

THE ART OF REMAINING BITTER

As the best dressmaker in the community, her mother worked for months in advance of the parade. The magistrate, Mrs. Couthaud, had already been in for her fitting. Mom had designed a glamorous, gold dress for her.

"Are you almost done, Sylvia?"

"Just about," she lied.

It was like this for her every school night. But for as long as she could remember, she had aspired to be better than her sister. She couldn't make everyone love her. She couldn't turn the magical age of twelve any faster. But she could figure out word problems, eventually. Then, one day, if they saved enough money, she would be in the University, studying art.

Mom spread a shimmering, bluish-gray fabric across her worktable in the adjacent family room. "Caralea needs space, too."

Sylvia eyed the expensive-looking fabric for Caralea's dress and wondered how many of her future college classes it could have paid for.

"We can share the table," Caralea said cheerfully.

She sat across from Sylvia, taking out a white, cloth banner and colorful markers.

"Only a few more days until your Bliss," Caralea said. "Aren't you excited?"

Sylvia considered asking Caralea what her friends thought about the experience. Could she tell her anything meaningful? But Sylvia didn't want to give her a chance to act all superior and older-sisterish. "Ashley said it's no big deal."

Caralea nodded, apparently nonplussed by Sylvia's lack of enthusiasm. She wrote out "Festival of Joy" in crooked, misshapen letters. Her markers made a scritching sound across the fabric.

Sylvia sighed at the distraction. She didn't need math to know that at this rate her homework would take hours.

HERO LOST: MYSTERIES OF DEATH AND LIFE

* * *

Later that night, her father went to bed early, exhausted from his long hours at the farm. Her mother continued to work on Caralea's gown. Last year, her dress was sleek and fitted with enormous shoulders that almost looked like folded wings. She wondered with a jealous stomach what her mother would create this year. It was hard to tell based on her sister's sketch.

Caralea colored more banners, her other homework long completed. When her sister took a break to consult with Mom about the hem length, Sylvia impulsively slipped a dark green marker under her tablet and carried it to the room she shared with her sister.

She wanted to document her negative feelings, to make a list of everything she hated. Soon, the hate would go away, and part of her didn't want it to. With Ashley walking around like a happy robot, Sylvia didn't trust her memory to hold. It felt important to capture the way she really felt before the procedure interfered.

The teachers had complete access to student computers, so that wasn't a safe place to record anything. She clutched the green marker, examining the space she shared with Caralea. They each had a dresser and a bed with a table next to it.

She opened a dresser drawer, rifled through her clothes. Some of the shirts were too small for her. As she turned each one inside-out, she focused on her unpleasant memories. Like the rude way that Maddox treated her at school. The torment in Mrs. Peters' eyes as they led her away. Ashley's lost grief. What would Sylvia lose? Her bitterness? She knew her mother loved Caralea more. Didn't she have a right to that anger? She wondered if she would even care about school without the jealousy that drove her.

THE ART OF REMAINING BITTER

The Bliss would take away her bad feelings. But recording them would make sure that she didn't forget. She wrote them in code, a different image on each shirt. The recent math problem she struggled to learn. A mean face for Maddox. An oval potato for Mrs. Peters' arrest. Last, she drew the hospital building where they had saved Caralea. Then she hid the marker under the dresser, where it could have rolled by accident.

* * *

Sylvia and Ashley walked to school together on Tuesday morning. It was another lovely day, and the city had an electrifying hum to it with the Festival approaching. People scurried around, mapping and marking parade routes, cleaning store windows, and hanging cheerful decorations.

Ashley didn't mention her mother.

After lunch, the sixth graders were in charge of arranging last year's banners into groups of four. Several classes gathered in the gym where they could spread the banners out. They pinned each quartet so that the eighth graders could then sew them into blankets for the elderly as part of their Family and Consumer Science class.

Sylvia took her time with the pile of banners her teacher, Mrs. Higgins, gave her. She tried to balance the colors in each group so that the resulting blankets would be something pretty. Next to her, Maddox haphazardly pinned his together.

Mrs. Higgins circulated around the gym, checking their progress. "Nice work, Sylvia. You have a good sense of composition," she said.

Sylvia smiled, but Maddox took that moment to knock over the container of pins, some of them landing dangerously close to her knees. He caught her eye long enough to let her know that the spill wasn't an accident. She wished she could pick up one

HERO LOST: MYSTERIES OF DEATH AND LIFE

of the pins and give him a poke in his scrawny arm.

Maybe she wasn't the only one. She heard Mrs. Higgins whispering to another teacher.

"The students are so much easier to handle after Bliss."

"When's his birthday?"

"Sunday," Mrs. Higgins said.

Two days after Sylvia's. Was Maddox counting down the days with dread, too?

* * *

Wednesday evening, Mom and Caralea were in total dress mode while Dad read his farm production reports. Sylvia retreated to her room to study in quiet.

"Come see," Mom called to her soon after. "Come see Caralea's gown."

Sylvia had at least another hour of homework to do. But she left stuff scattered across her bed and dragged herself into the family room.

"Wow!" She couldn't help herself. The gown was the complete opposite of last year's sleek one. This dress was full, with each layer getting wider towards the bottom. The color looked striking against her sister's skin.

As Caralea twirled with delight, the bottom edge of the cascading fabric nearly touching the walls. Dad clapped his hands.

Mom beamed, proud of her work. "Thank you. The top fabric was expensive, but to create the fullness—look!" She lifted the shimmering material.

Sylvia gasped. Underneath the beautiful blue-gray was layer after layer of old clothes. She caught sight of some of her T-shirts, the ones she had used to record her emotions.

"My clothes!" she yelled. "You didn't even ask me! Some of those shirts were mine."

"Don't be silly," Mom said. "You've outgrown those things. You never even wear them anymore."

THE ART OF REMAINING BITTER

"But they were mine!" Suddenly, Sylvia began to yell. She let out scream after scream, louder and louder.

Dad jumped up. "Stop! Someone will call the police."

But Sylvia couldn't stop. She shrieked until a forceful knock sounded at the door, until the big, red-haired man gripped her arm tightly.

"Come with me."

"No, please," Dad said. "She's only days away from Bliss. It's this Friday."

"She needs to be confined," Officer Reed said.

Mom whimpered.

Sylvia knew the term. If pre-Bliss children were completely out of control, they took them somewhere—no one ever told where—and held them until their procedure. Bliss never occurred before twelve, but confinement was a way to keep everyone safe until then, they said. Sylvia only knew one boy who had been confined—an eleven-year-old last year who pulled the legs off bugs and collected the dead bodies in his dresser under his clothes.

"That won't be necessary," Dad said.

The policeman didn't look convinced.

Still in her gown, Caralea stepped forward to stand next to Sylvia. "Please," she said. "It was my fault. Please don't punish her."

Sylvia was afraid to breathe during his long hesitation. Without a doubt, he recognized her sister, the special one.

"This Friday?" he confirmed in a no-nonsense voice.

"Yes," Sylvia whispered.

"For you, it won't be a moment too soon."

* * *

Thursday evening, Sylvia waited nervously for everyone to leave so she could recreate her memory

HERO LOST: MYSTERIES OF DEATH AND LIFE

list. Dad was at work, and Mom took Caralea to a parade-planning meeting. Sylvia could finally be alone in her room. She needed an alternative to the clothes, something that wouldn't be easily taken away. Her eyes settled on the bedside table she'd had forever. After clearing it off, she flipped it over. The rectangle underneath made for a sturdy drawing space. Sylvia sketched her images as small as possible. She changed Maddox to a pointy pin. After she finished the hospital, she included one final image: her sister's gown. She drew it in two halves, one full and pretty, and the other made of rags covered in frowny faces.

The next morning, Dad took her to the edge of the woods. It was a rite of passage, parents letting their children walk the last portion on their own.

"What if I can't find it?" she asked.

Dad smiled. "You can't miss the medical facility. It's a sprawling rectangular building." He urged her forward.

The sunlight peeked through the trees, casting shadows along the way. It was normal to be afraid, right? Would she lose her fear after the Bliss?

Moving slowly, she looked for signs of another trail. Brown pine needles covered the ground between the trees, and there was no obvious path. Then, on her left, she saw it: a flutter of white fabric, as if someone had cut off a strip of a Festival banner. She stopped. Kona had been telling the truth!

"Sylvia!" Someone called to her from the direction of the hospital. "Sylvia! This way, dear!"

She walked toward the voice. A woman beckoned to her from outside the hospital doors. "I'm Mrs. McKenzie," she said. "I'm here to check you in."

Sylvia glanced back one more time before she was ushered inside. Mrs. McKenzie took her into a sterile-looking room with two metal chairs and explained the procedure. Sylvia nodded at the appropriate pauses, but she had a hard time listening. She was thinking about the fabric fluttering in the breeze.

"The doctor will be in shortly. It won't hurt at all," the woman reassured her. "Just a little pinch."

When she woke, a new peace radiated through her. It was deeper than the relaxation she felt at night, when the house was quiet and she was on the verge of sleep. This was a blissful emptiness, like the blank page on her computer screen.

Dad bought her chocolate ice cream on the way back. She wanted to go home and take a nap, but Dad insisted that she attend school.

She arrived in time for math. This is important, Sylvia thought. I have to focus. But the beauty of the blue sky and the occasional puffy cloud distracted her. The hours in school flew by. On the way home, she and Ashley made plans to meet at the candy store the next day so Sylvia could get chocolate before the parade.

After dinner, Caralea modeled her finished dress. "You look..." Sylvia paused. "Beautiful." Her sister smiled, and Sylvia took a quick inventory of how she felt. No resentment. No jealousy. If her previous emotions were like the volcanos they studied in science, now they were a mere wisp of smoke. Or maybe something soft and green, like the plants she loved at the farm. These emotions confused her. She'd never felt kindly when it came to Caralea.

Sylvia escaped to her room as soon as she could. Once she was alone, she quietly flipped over her bedside table to study the symbols she had recorded. They seemed foreign, like something from another life. Grabbing the green marker, she held it over her sketches, feeling compelled to cross them out, to obscure them with a pretty drawing of leaves on a vine.

She touched the marker's tip to the picture of the

hospital, hesitating.

Maybe she wouldn't cover the drawings just yet.

Instead, she hurriedly drew the gate and the trail to the Bliss hospital, adding a line to the left where she saw the flutter. It would serve as a tiny map of the path in the woods. Maybe, another day, she would go back. The idea felt like a spark, like fireworks in an otherwise tranquil sky.

Savoring the feeling, she replaced the cap on the marker. Then she put it back among her sister's supplies and joined her family.

The End

Yvonne Ventresca's latest young adult novel, the psychological thriller BLACK FLOWERS, WHITE LIES (Sky Pony Press, 2016) was listed at the top of Buzzfeed's must-read new young adult books for fall. Her debut YA novel, PANDEMIC, won a 2015 Crystal Kite Award from the Society of Children's Book Writers and Illustrators. Yvonne's other works include the short story "Escape to Orange Blossom," which was selected for the dystopian anthology PREP FOR DOOM, along with two nonfiction books, PUBLISHING (Careers for the 21st Century) and AVRIL LAVIGNE (People in the News). Yvonne blogs about writing and the creative life on her website: www.YvonneVentresca.com/blog.html
You can also find her:
www.twitter.com/YvonneVentresca
www.instagram.com/YvonneVentresca

Of Words and Swords
By Tyrean Martinson

"Oh, my lady, forsooth, this is how you remind me of—"

"Stop that racket, Maud!" The shout echoed from the back of the pub, followed by a crock full of ale that landed on the floor at Maud's feet and splattered up on his dark pants.

"Now, there's no cause to waste Master Ghent's fine ale," stated Maud, bending down to scoop up the mug before it emptied all of its contents. He managed to get a few drops in his mouth, more than he'd had to drink in hours.

In his peripheral vision, Maud could see a hairy fist headed in the direction of his face. He ducked, twisted, and landed a punch in his opponent's saggy gut.

The hairy-handed man went down with a grunt, his eyes glassy.

Maud stepped around him, wound his way through the tables of jeering patrons, and approached the barkeep. "I don't think this is the right crowd for my poetry, Master Ghent."

Master Ghent shook his craggy face and took the mug from him. "It's never going to be the right crowd, Maud. You best pick up your swords again and leave the poetry to the bards."

"When I defeated the Dragon Horde, King Tristan granted me gold and told me to go after my heart's desire. I've always wanted to be a poet."

Ghent's mouth quirked at the edges, but he quickly wiped at his mouth with the back of his hand.

HERO LOST: MYSTERIES OF DEATH AND LIFE

"I think the King wanted you to marry his daughter and become one of his knights, not spend your days writing poetry in the dusty attic of Widow Larkin's place."

"It's a garret, not an attic."

"Either way, it's no place for the finest fighter of our land."

Maud pressed his lips together. "An attic is a cramped space used to store unused items whilst a garret is a dark abode that feeds the soul of a poet."

Ghent grunted. "I don't think the dark suits you."

Maud glanced down at his crumpled scroll containing the words he had spent hours trying to perfect. "I can hear the music in the words; I just don't understand why no one else can."

"Music needs rhythm and the lyre, not fancy words and sighs. Trust me, I know good music and it sets the patrons to drinking my casks dry."

Maud sighed. Did no one understand his desire to capture words in the epic dance of emotion and story? Did everyone only want to listen to silly stories, gossip, and music with bawdy lyrics? He twisted the scroll in his hands and stuffed it into the small bag of papers he carried at his side instead of the twin swords that had earned him fame. He bid Ghent goodnight, and wandered out of the tavern into the street.

The moon, heavy with harvest light, hung deep in the sky, beckoning praise and…Maud's musings were interrupted by the clatter of horse's hooves and the strained shouts of men.

"Fire! Fire at the castle! The Horde has returned! Men to arms!"

Maud swiveled on his feet to face the castle on the hill across the river. Flames engulfed the west side of the castle, and a huge winged form flew between the bright fire and the river.

OF WORDS AND SWORDS

Maud stood for a moment, and then he rushed to his room above Widow Larkin's house. He had his own stairway entrance outside and he climbed the stairs at a run, threw open his door, and rushed to his locked chest. Fumbling for a moment, he withdrew the key from the chain on his chest. He closed his eyes, knowing what it would mean to open the lock and knowing what it might mean if he didn't.

He bid farewell to the music of words within his mind and opened the lock. His two sword—Thunder and Lightning—lay inside. He had named them when he forged them, not realizing then how powerful the names might make them.

With shaking fingers, he took off the bag of scrolls and placed them at the end of the chest. He withdrew his armor—lightweight for movement but given the ability to withstand dragon-fire by Sorceress Elia. He strapped it on with deft movements, and then took out his sword-belt and fastened it around him. With Thunder and Lightning in their sheaths, he donned his light helmet and the greaves for his arms and legs.

Maud gazed at his bag of scrolls one more time before he closed the chest and locked it, returning the key to rest around his neck. "I will return to you," he promised, holding onto the key. With regret, he stood, exited his garret, and raced down the steps into the street.

Villagers scattered in all directions, some to the castle to help, some away in fear, and some on errands that seemed inexplicable to Maud. No matter. He ran to the fight, taking the shortest route he knew to Stone Bridge, aptly name for its construction and ability to withstand attacks.

At the bridge, Maud ran with a trickle of armed men toward the castle. No one spoke as he passed them, but most gave him room as he overtook the group. His long strides slowed as he reached the upward slope of Castle Hill and he lost his breath. Where had his stamina gone? He slowed to a mere walk. Those he had overtaken now passed him, and some of them sneered.

"Poets don't fight dragons."

"Bards should go flock with the chickens."

Maud ground his teeth together, but then unclenched them so he could breathe easier. He knew more than they how words could help in a battle; it was what had convinced him that he could be a Bard.

As he neared the top of Castle Hill, the heat sucked the air out of his lungs and made his face burn. He heard the screaming of men and women dying. The dragon flew silently, flaming death to all it encountered.

Maud wished he could gain more speed, but he realized his days of writing poetry in a garret had robbed him of his former strength. Nerves and excitement fueled his initial haste. His veins still thrummed with anticipation, but his body needed to be held in check for the actual battle. He would have to be quick.

Close the castle, Maud paused by the shadow of a well-house. He didn't like skulking when a fight ensued, but he needed a plan.

The dragon attacking the castle appeared to be alone, but he also seemed to be one of the ancients; an older and larger dragon with a few battle scars striping his sides. It was bound to be clever, probably more clever than Maud.

So, that left Maud with the oldest attack in the world. He exited his temporary shelter and shouted up at the beast.

"Vile fiend that sets the castle alight, come and fight me! I am your enemy, not the soft nobles whom you have killed!"

The dragon heard him over the cries of his victims

and paused, beating his wings hard to keep him in flight, searching for Maudlin in the castle's keep.

In those split seconds, Maud threw Lightning at the beast, sending the sword in a rotating arc of metal toward its breast. "Strike, Lightning, strike the foul beast with thy majestic light, from the power of the heavens to the blight of the land!"

The sword's metal took on the appearance of white fire as it thrust itself toward the dragon, but the dragon shifted easily out of the way as the sword's light faltered and flew into the flames surrounding the castle.

Maud groaned. His back, shoulder, and arm ached from that move. The words had failed him.

The dragon flew at him, spewing orange flames in his direction. Maud ran into the well-house and jumped into the shaft, feet first, his hands scrambling for purchase against the stony sides of the well. Several feet down, his right hand caught the edge of a rock and his left scrabbled for another handhold.

Fire enveloped the roof of the well-house, and the entire building went up in a whoosh of smoke and destruction above his head.

Maud cowered in the well-shaft, not sure how he was going to get out, much less fight the dragon. Words had never failed him so badly. Lightning was gone. Thunder was at his side, but what could he hope to do with it if his words failed again?

Flames shot down the well, but didn't reach Maud. Whether his armor or just luck protected him, he didn't know. The flames came again and again, and he still clung to the crevices in the wall, trembling until his fingers slipped.

He fell, his arms flailing and scraping against the sides of the well. His feet plunged into the water, and he sank down into the cold. He crawled against the water, fought it, until he surfaced. He was at the bottom of the well. The dragon spewed flames and more flames, but he was safe...as long as he didn't drown.

Treading water was never Maud's favorite pasttime, but he knew how to keep himself alive. He circled his arms slowly, tilted his head back, and felt for purchase against the stones of the well with his boots. There, a small ledge on the right. It would keep him afloat for hours.

Above him, the dragon continued to send flames down the well. Aside from heat on his face, Maud was outside of the dragon's range.

At some point during the night, the dragon stopped trying to roast him. The sky above the well revealed an orange glow. The whole castle keep was probably on fire.

Maud wept for a moment. He reached out to the side of the well, stretching away from his tiny foothold. Half bent, he was able to bridge the other side. His cold, aching arms didn't want to climb, but otherwise he would drown. He kicked off the stone wall, his arms burning, his legs aching. He only looked up.

With trembling arms and legs, he finally reached the top of the well. He hauled himself out into the miserable ruins of the burnt well-house. The stones under him were still uncomfortably warm and smoldering beams blocked his way out. He cut strips from his wet shirt and wrapped them around his feet. The shortest distance with the least wreckage in his way would take five steps through embers and ruins. It was the only way. He picked his path and stumbled out into the castle square with only slightly singed toes. He wrapped his feet again in wet cloth and gazed around at the destruction.

The castle keep gaped like an open wound. No wooden structures remained. The charred stones gave testament to the dragon's wrath. A small group of people stood outside the front of the castle. Maud trudged toward them. They circled him with confusion, despair, and anger etched on their faces.

Princess Gwen, dressed only in a nightshift and robe, glared at him. "Where were you, Maud? Where were you when my father died? Why didn't you fight the dragon? Were you writing poetry?"

"No," Maud said softly. "I tried to attack but my assault failed."

"You should be dead." Gwen turned to one of her remaining knights who had survived the attack. "Put him in the dungeon."

"He would die, your majesty, and we need this skills."

"No, we don't."

Maud forced his aching muscles to bend to a kneeling position. "Please, your majesty, let me track the dragon to its lair and avenge good King Thrace's death."

"As long as that puts you out of my sight and your chances of death are high, you may. But do not expect a reward, poet." She made poet sound like a nasty word.

Maud glanced at the others, who clenched their fists and turned their noses away from him. He walked away from the crowd toward the bridge. Along the way, he passed wreckage and the dead. He knew he should help bury them, but it was unlikely that anyone would accept his assistance. He kept his head down, not looking up at all. The dragon's swath of destruction would be a trail he couldn't miss, at least until the beast grew bored.

When he crossed the bridge, Maud came to a halt. The dragon had burned the houses to the foundations. Widow Larkin's place, his chest of poems, and the pub—all gone. But he had to cross through the village to follow the dragon's path. He wasn't sure he possessed the courage to face the villagers, so he crossed the road and walked into Farmer Giles' fields. He could skirt around the village that way.

Of course, it wasn't that easy to avoid his responsibility. The guilt of it weighed down on him. He had been so sure all the dragons were gone or at least those that would harass his home. He had thought he could lay down his swords and rest. But, the words had slipped through his fingers, and a dragon destroyed his home.

When he was almost clear of the village, two figures approached him in the field. He couldn't avoid contact without being obvious, so he allowed them to draw nearer. It was Master Ghent and Widow Larkin.

Maud stopped. He didn't know what to say to them.

"Lad, I don't know what happened, but I did hear that you needed supplies for your quest," Master Ghent stated. He held up a carry-sack that bulged at the sides and a pair of boots.

"And, you will need someone to watch your back in the evenings," Widow Larkin stated, with her hands gripping a stout staff.

"No."

"Maud, don't be a fool. You need boots, supplies, and help."

"I'll take the boots and the supplies, not the help. You've both already helped me enough."

"Well, I'm not coming along with the pub's cellar one of the only safe stores of food in the village, but I wish you both well." He handed Maud the bag and the boots and clapped him on the back. "Do us proud again, Maud."

Maud nodded and yanked on the boots. He ignored Widow Larkin, which was harder to do than usual. He noticed, out of the corner of his eyes, that she had traded her usual black dress for a pair of black pants and a black shirt with a black journey cloak. Her boots looked like the sort one used for travel or riding, and they were scuffed with use.

When he looked up, he noticed she wasn't wearing her usual glasses either and her gray hair wasn't in a bun. In fact, she had cut her hair into short, wavy white and gray locks that hung around her face and her eyes were an azure color that he had only seen once before in his life. "You're a sorceress."

She nodded. "A woman living alone in a village must have her resources, if she is to live."

"But the dragon?"

She sighed. "I'm not that powerful. I'm more like a hedge witch than a sorceress. That's how I came to live in the village and not the castle. I'm not the type to impress kings or protect kingdoms. I do smaller magic, and like you, I have fallen out of practice. It was easier to be simply Widow Larkin from South Bend who teaches the school-children their lessons and takes in strays."

"Like me?"

"Yes."

He gazed at her with more attention now. "How old are you? And what kind of spells do you know that might help me?"

"My age is not important. I have minor control over the humidity in the air, small plants and animals, and I make a few healing tonics. I can't call lightning, control a dragon, or heal any serious injuries."

"All right, then you may come, if you truly wish it, but know that I may be walking to my death. One of my swords is gone, and I may have lost control over the other."

"Isn't that a matter of practice?"

"Yes and no. I learned that words may have power in a battle. Usually, when I call out my swords' names, they strike true. That didn't happen today."

HERO LOST: MYSTERIES OF DEATH AND LIFE

"Interesting." She hummed low in her throat for a moment and pointed along the path of the dragon's fire. "Let us go, then."

They fell into a quiet rhythm, not speaking for several hours.

Maud realized just how useless he had let his body grow as his feet began to ache, then his calves. However, he didn't want to admit that to Widow Larkin who seemed to be walking next to him without any effort.

When they reached River Westerly, they discovered the wooden bridge burned to ash by the dragon. Thankfully, the water level was low. Maud took off his boots and waded partway into the river, and then turned back to help the Widow.

She walked on the water, with her boots on, and passed him as he gawked.

"It's a minor trick and I can't share it unfortunately," she said as he floundered up onto the other side.

"Oh." He couldn't think of anything else to say. Widow Larkin was turning out to be more than he imagined her to be.

"I don't know about you, but my feet are aching. I'm going to attempt a call if you don't mind resting for a moment."

"What are you calling?"

"Horses."

Maud sat down on a boulder by the river and decided to inspect the supplies while surreptitiously watching Widow Larkin. The bag held a whole wheel of cheese, two loaves of bread, a small cutting knife, a packet of salt, and a jug of sweet mead. It was a traveler's treasure trove.

Meanwhile, Widow Larkin closed her eyes, held out her hands, and started humming a rollicking melody that almost sounded like horses' hooves running on the grass.

OF WORDS AND SWORDS

Nothing happened right away, but then her humming deepened.

Maud heard real hoof-beats trotting through the grass. Four horses whirled to a stop, circling the Widow.

Widow Larkin changed her tune, holding out her hand.

A bay mare came towards her, whuffing softly. Then, the black mare came to her, eyeing her curiously.

The other two nickered a question, and the Widow seemed to answer them. They wandered away while the bay and the black stayed by her side.

"Surely, fine horses like these have owners."

Widow Larkin smiled and cocked her head to one side. "I only take what I need and only if the horse is willing."

Maud found himself speechless again. The black mare blew into his hair, and he reached up to rub the horses' jawline.

Within minutes, they were both astride the mares, riding bareback along the dragon's trail of fire through the countryside.

* * *

They traveled for three days, staying only in a tiny hamlet one night at the urging of a farmer who allowed them to use his barn and gave them food. He only wanted their promise to kill the dragon in return. They agreed. Maud hoped they could fulfill their promise.

The dragon's fiery trail of ruin ended on the fourth day in a path that led up the foothills of Mount Hargut.

"I think it wants us to follow it," stated Widow Larkin.

"Yes, it does. It wants to kill anyone that would challenge it." Maud leaned back in his saddle. "The question is: how far is it from the end of its trail?"

"What do you mean?"

"Dragons love mountains and caves, so somewhere high up on Mount Hargut would be an obvious place for its lair. But this dragon is ancient and battle-scarred. It may not speak like a human, but it is clever. The dragon may be anywhere between here and the highest peak of Mount Hargut."

"How will we know where it is?"

"Normally, I would simply take a side trail, taking it slow and quiet. Dragons have a distinct odor to them, so I would know when I drew near. However," he glanced at Widow Larkin, "I've never had a sorceress with me before."

"What can I do?"

"Could you ask a small animal, like a rabbit or a bird, how close the dragon is?"

"I can call them and ask them to obey, but I can't ask small animals actual questions. Their minds don't understand mine."

"Oh, well, I guess we'll do it the old-fashioned way then." He jumped off of his black mare to the ground. "Can you tell the horses to go back to that farmer's place?"

"Yes, horses are intelligent enough for that." She looked down at him. "We have to walk?"

Maud bit his lip. He realized that he had grown used to her company. "Actually, we don't have to walk. I have to walk. You could ride back to the farmer's land and stay with the horses until I finish."

"No." She jumped off of her horse.

"Widow Larkin, you've been kind, helpful, and altogether wonderful to have on this quest, but I'm the dragon-slayer. You are not."

"My name is Emilie." She blushed, and her hair changed color, from white to reddish brown.

"You're not a widow."

OF WORDS AND SWORDS

"No."

"And, I am a terrible poet."

"You are a warrior poet, not a peaceful poet or a romantic poet. The words you use can fuel your warcraft because you have a bit of magic in you, but that is all."

Maud sighed. "I don't know if I can kill this dragon. I only have Thunder." He put his hand on the sword's hilt.

"We will work together."

"I don't want you killed."

"I don't want to be killed either. We'll have to make sure it doesn't happen." Emilie hummed quietly and slapped her horse on its rump.

The horses galloped away, back where they had come from.

Maud closed his eyes, but felt a smile forming on his lips. "Away we go to battle, the Widow and I, she has her power, and I have Thunder at my side."

Emilie chuckled. "Not fine poetry, but it will work for what we have ahead. Plain language is best in battle."

"And you would know this?"

"I have my past. If you're able to keep me alive, you might get to hear it." She smiled at him and stepped off the trail.

Maud followed her lead off the side of the path, through some light undergrowth, and up into first rocky boulders on the side of the mountain. A rank odor reached them on a small breeze. Maud touched Emilie's arm and she stopped. He crouched and pointed in the direction of the breeze. She nodded.

He led this time, crawling slowly over the rough terrain, keeping his progress silent.

Emilie came close behind.

As the scent grew stronger, it changed slightly. Maud hesitated, trying to figure out what was different.

HERO LOST: MYSTERIES OF DEATH AND LIFE

Behind them, a tree shook.

Maud grabbed Emilie and rolled them both over three feet and in between two boulders that leaned against one another. She stared at him with wide eyes, her shirt torn slightly at the elbow from the rough passage. He held his finger to his lips and started picturing words in his mind, simple words for battle.

The dragon approached with heavy steps, swinging its head back and forth to taste the scents in the air.

Maud slowly drew his sword from its sheath and whispered his words to it. "Thunder roll. Thunder rumble." He held the sword ready and waited, saying the words again and again in his mind, not allowing any other thoughts into him. The world narrowed to the dragon and him.

As the creature stepped in front of their hiding place, Maud rushed out and plunged his sword into the gap between its front leg and its armored chest. "Thunder roll. Thunder rumble."

Behind him, Emilie began to sing in another language. The music hit percussive notes that matched Maud's words.

The blade shook violently in his hands, but he held on as it dug into the dragon's armpit.

The dragon roared in pain and thrashed, but Maud held to the sword's pommel and repeated his phrase over and over again. The blade bit deeper into the dragon's chest, thrumming with power.

The dragon arched its back, slammed its feet to the ground, and flung its wings to the sides.

The humidity of the air around them rose, and clouds gathered overhead until rain began to fall. The dragon roared, flapped its wet wings, and struggled to take off.

Maud still held tight, his legs dangling, thrown into the dragon's chest by its flailing. He shouted. "Thunder roll! Thunder rumble. Lightning strike!"

OF WORDS AND SWORDS

The clouds above them rumbled and flashed.

The dragon launched from the ground, flying at an odd, desperate angle not far from the ground, but Maud hung onto his sword, still shouting his battle cry, over and over again.

The clouds cracked open and a bright flash struck the dragon.

The lightning coursed through the beast and hit Maud. He clenched his hands harder around the pommel of the sword and screamed as the dragon fell to the earth.

Blackness surrounded him.

Nightmares came and were chased away by a soft humming.

Gentle hands tended his burns.

Rain came and went. A pattering fell on some kind of shelter.

Finally, Maud opened his eyes and could see.

He rested on a cot, in a tent. Emilie sat near him. On the ground by her side, two swords lay sheathed. Somehow, Lightning had come back to him. But that didn't really matter.

"Emilie," he whispered.

She gazed down at him and smiled. "Welcome back, my warrior poet."

He smiled and reached for her. "Lady, you remind me of who I really am. I was lost and I wandered, but now I am home."

She leaned down and kissed him with soft lips, and he knew his words had worked magic, at least once.

The End

Tyrean Martinson, an everyday writer, likes to write in jeans and old Christian concert t-shirts while drinking copious amounts of tea and coffee, preferably served up in her Tinkerbell or Eeyore mugs (these are 16oz mugs, not wee cups). She teaches writing classes to home-school teens and she writes fantasy, science fiction, space opera, poetry, experimental hint fiction, and writing books.

www.tyreanswritingspot.blogspot.com/
www.twitter.com/TyreanMartinson
www.facebook.com/tyrean

Breath Between Seconds
By L. Nahay

The sunlight is scorching, whiting out my vision. It stuns me, startles me off guard. I take a breath and it becomes a gasp, a gulp for air. I can't remember why I would have been holding my breath. My lungs burn, so I know that I had been. I throw my head back to grab more air, except that my head doesn't move. I seem to be lying on my back, with something pressed up against the back of my head, keeping it in place. I do it again: breathe. A third time. Deep and desperate.

Once adequately re-oxygenated, the blanket covering my senses is pulled away, and pain pulsates from the back of my head down. My body is a cacophony of parts, disjointed and discomfited parts. I lose the rhythm of in, out, unable to focus past the overwhelming throb. I close my eyes and refocus my breaths. One, two, one right after the other. This is good. It's good.

The pain lessons enough that I can think again. It occurs to me to shield my eyes. I lift my hand, but it had been pressed to my side, which explodes in pain and something else. I clamp it back to where it was, trying not to think about why my fingers are sticky.

My ears pop. Now that there's silence, I realize that they had been ringing. They equalize further, and I catch the sound of ragged breathing. It's a labored effort that rattles and is excruciating to hear, a wet gurgle that mixes with the struggle for air. I take a breath, exhale, listening. No, it's not from me. From my left. I turn my head away from the scorch above me to find the source, counting the seconds in between each horrible *in*...

...*out.*

Five seconds.

I see nothing. I hadn't been breathing, and I hadn't been hearing. Now I'm not seeing.

No, I see black. Damn hair. Always coming undone no matter how I tie it back. I tried cutting it short once, short like the men, but that ended up feeling wrong. I grew it out and thought that when it reached my chin, it would be better. I'd look feminine again and it'd be out of my way. But that length was worse than long. I couldn't pull it away at all. It was constantly in my eyes. Nothing more intrusive and aggravating than trying to spar while being blinded by your own damn hair. So, I let it continue to grow. Mid-back now. It's boring, but easier to throw into a tail or a braid. It's the only feminine thing about me. My body is as lean and muscular as any male soldier. I stride when I walk. Put me in armor and you wouldn't know me from the rest of my male counterparts. Me in a dress is awkwardly funny. But that's fine. I'm proud of my body. It's mine. I chose it. I worked to perfect it, to be strong, to be fast, to be a capable fighter, a trustworthy soldier. What use is it to look good in a dress?

Nine seconds.

I almost lift my hand. I try the other, but that one is also pressed over my side. Heavens, my body hurts. Every discomfited, disjointed part. I huff out a strong exhale of air to blow the hair out of my eyes. Not much happens. I try again, feeling foolish. I haven't blown at my hair since I was a child. It feels petty.

Silver. I see silver through the black of my sweat-dampened hair. I roll my eyes at myself. My helmet, of course. I've got to take it off. I think about my hands but catch myself in time. I tilt my head back,

BREATH BETWEEN SECONDS

which is in the direction of my right shoulder. My helmet grinds against something else made of metal, catches, and stops. I lift my head a fraction and wince in a breath, move my head back a little more. Then forward again, back some more, using whatever my helmet is catching on to help dislodge it little by little until it is removed. I hold my breath as it rolls away. Clatters. Falls. A long way. I must be lying on a hill.

Eleven seconds.

I exhale. That was arduous. I keep my eyes closed, grateful for the respite from the sun, and take a slow inhale. But abruptly I stop, holding my breath again at the smell of blood. Death. I feel death. And someone else's breath shivering along my nose and lips, teasing my tangled hair. The gurgling is closer than I'd thought. I keep my eyes closed, my heart racing in panic. Who am I lying beside? Why? I count his breaths again, letting mine out in small, calculated increments.

Twelve seconds.

My hands are holding my side in. I try to reach my senses out, as if my swords and knives will speak back and tell me where I've dropped them. Silence. And rattling, gurgling breathing. I whisper a prayer to the gods and open my eyes.

Before me is a man, his brown eyes staring sightless into mine. Boring into me. I stop breathing, waiting for him to inhale again. I know him. Following that recognition is the complete awareness that we are lying atop a mound of bodies on the southern edge of this month's battlefield. That this is the three thousandth, two hundred sixteenth day of war–of this particular war. And I, a lieutenant of the House of Vili, delivered the death blow to the House of Dochure's crown prince, Danu. The man struggling to breathe before me.

I won the war. That is why there is silence. I

brought him down, the fighting stopped, and everyone retreated back. We are the only two left. He's barely alive. How alive am I? I try to move, but my legs don't respond.

Danu inhales deep and louder than before, the suddenness of it jarring me. I flinch, feel the movement course down my body in an explosive echo of pain along every thread of nerve. His eyes are coherent and seeing. Soft, brown eyes locked on the only breathing person nearby. I can't fault him for not wanting to die alone. Rots for him that the only one nearby is the one who killed him. My pulse quickens, but I do not look away from him.

His eyes aren't calculating and detached as they'd been when we'd fought. They aren't bitter, or enraged, or shocked. They just are. I decide that his eyelashes and the hair beneath his black helmet is also black. Right now, he is covered in his blood. It's spilling out of him from his mouth, his ears and nose, his many wounds. His fingers are spread over the gash along his throat, hoping to contain the spillage. But it's futile. It was the last slice I'd given him. Overkill after the sword through his torso and the dagger to his spine. I'd been trained well: never assume that the last was enough.

Blood bubbles up from between his lips and quietly slips out the downed corner of his mouth. With a start, I realize how close we are. Half an arm span. Close enough that we can feel the other's breath. Close enough that I could wipe his blood away. Would it help him breathe easier?

My hands are holding my side in.

Sixteen seconds.

Danu exhales. I smile, sigh out my breath.

We were allies once, our Houses. For centuries. Then one day, someone decided war would be fun. I don't know who began it. I know little about Danu personally, some about his family. I've never been to his region. Maybe it looks like mine. Maybe it's in the mountains here. Maybe by the sea. I know about Dochure House's part in this battle for the land between our Houses; land neither of us owns or needs to own, land previously inhabited by creatures we've since massacred.

It's always something, isn't it? A sacred talisman, magic, mining rights for some powerful gemstone someone's sure they've located, someone daring to love a forbidden other. Now it's for an extension of boundaries to tack onto what was previously obtained with previous generations' bloodshed.

I flick my eyes back to Danu. Our fight is starting to remember me, replacing the pain with numbing exhaustion. This at least feels better. I probably hit my head when I fell. That would explain the throbbing. Concussive, maybe. I shouldn't allow my eyes to close. I count several of my breaths. Irregular. Three seconds. One second. Two seconds.

Twenty-three seconds between Danu's.

I think his family, his House, his people will mourn him. He's the eldest of five, the only son. His sisters never married. His devotion to them was so widely known that my side took advantage of it and attacked all four in a synchronized attack one day last week. Three were killed, and one was delivered to my Prince as a trophy. The Elites of my legion had been overheard recapping the secret mission. The tale had quickly spread through the ranks and then into the populace, igniting an outcry against such barbarism. The people chanted and raged outside the gates of the House for days, but none from within acknowledged, addressed, or denied the rumors. I was vocal against it among my circle. I was on the tail end of leave then–last week? Only last week?–and had stood outside the gates in civilian attire, screaming and chanting until my voice was lost with theirs. But my voice is meaningless. A couple days later, my orders came in and I marched out obediently. Nothing changed for those women. The stolen princess' only rescue is currently bleeding out beside me. I won the war for the side that resorted to using women as pawns and currency. Who am I to shout out about morals and what should be permissible in war?

What have we been fighting over? Land? Really? Princesses were murdered or sold, hundreds of thousands of soldiers have slaughtered each other, and I attacked a prince...for property rights. Now that we've won, my House won't be content. They'll turn on an ally and demand something else. Ownership of the sky and sun, power over all the Houses, some enchanted tiara or tree branch a doomed child of an insignificant farmer unearths.

Thirty seconds.

Danu takes a breath and I collapse in relief within my skin and armor.

Maybe his sisters had guards, and maybe they were all afraid to fight back. My Prince-and-General has garnered a supreme, unquestionable reputation as being a ferocious soldier with an insatiable lust for blood and violence and pain. So much so, that his counsel keeps him under heavy guard during all battles so as to prevent his atrocity. It's been said that his rage would be delivered to all within a fifty-mile league, should my esteemed Prince-and-General be unleashed.

Danu blinks, slow. A gush of blood falls from his mouth, yet he doesn't cough. My heart speeds up with fear. His pain has finally fled his consciousness, and his face has relaxed out of contortion. He is a handsome man. This saddens me, his handsomeness combined with my piecemeal, post-battle measure of him. It weighs me down into the bodies we are thrown over. I bet he is honorable. He knew my gender when I attacked him, and he did not twist it against me. What if he dies? I wait for his eyes to open again, but they don't. What thoughts are coursing through his mind? His tattered family, no doubt. How his parents have lost everything in a week. His wife. Oh gods, what if they have children? What did I do?

What if he dies–of course he will. *I killed him.* I feel guilty. I want to tell him that he didn't fail. He had fought me expertly. Graceful. Precise. Silent. He never gloated. Never goaded. He took no pleasure in the fight, in the blows, in the attempt to kill me first. His eyes showed thought and reflex, not the greedy delight I have seen in other opponents' or comrades' eyes. No boast, no sense of unquestioned righteousness and rarely-earned glory as my own Prince-and-General carries. In another life, I'd have thought Danu good, I think.

"I'm sorry," I tell him.

His mouth quirks up in a smile.

And then he dies without a final breath.

"I'm sorry," I repeat.

I turn my head away from him and stare up at the sky. It's not so bright anymore. I'm not in as much pain anymore, either. I don't need to breathe quite as much or as strong as moments ago. That could be good. I'll rest awhile longer, then try to get up. I should probably rejoin my troupe. In awhile. They won't care whether or not I return, or when. Soldiers vanish, get injured, are captured, die. Every single day. Three thousand, two hundred sixteen days.

What was I thinking? Deciding to kill this man?

I recall that moment, watching Danu swinging two massive swords against a horde of my troupe; on his own, a General-Prince surrounded by his enemy. He'd brought each of my comrades down, and it didn't faze me. I couldn't put my awe away. I've never

HERO LOST: MYSTERIES OF DEATH AND LIFE

seen someone fight like him–this man with no battle reputation, no preceding rumor on his profound skill. Or his grace, precision, silence.

But that's the thing with rumors. Spoken or absent, they are usually a fabrication.

The way to him was cleared with everyone fallen, and my Prince-and-General Petinst had cowered in his blown shelter within the shade of the trees, incapable of claiming the fight reserved for him. Prince-and-General. Both men hold the same rank and title and family empowerment, but they are vastly different men. All the surrounding soldiers had averted their attention and continued to fight within their ranks outside an invisible perimeter beyond Danu. I alone moved. There was no plan, no real intent. I am not the most-skilled fighter. I had no desire or need for glory or my own reputation boost. Attacking Danu would never elevate my rank. It will most likely, now that I can see forward, warrant my assassination.

My chance of success should have been zero. But I could not pretend a reason to avoid. The way was clear, the mission was there before me, so I had moved. I had caught him unaware as his blind spot faced me, and had landed a blow across his left side before he'd spun around and met me. Petinst was whisked away from his ruined hiding spot by his retinue of armored guards.

Coward isn't a word anyone has ever dared speak. Neither is incompetent. No comments have been made about his inadequate level of intelligence, or the lunacy of his rank as general. But he is the Prince of our House, inserted into the military as a general after 'years of intensive, very private one-on-one training'. He was promptly awarded his parent-appointed high counsel.

He'll claim this victory, be handed the crown one day soon.

BREATH BETWEEN SECONDS

I start to laugh. It's a choking laugh that fills me again with sharp, all-over pain. Maybe I should have thought a little bit about the outcome of attacking Danu before I'd done it.

There's voices and movement, and I go silent. I look over to Danu, only he's still dead. The blood from his mouth and nose is dried and dark. His throat has stopped bleeding. The hand that had been holding it together has fallen to lay between us. All his blood has abandoned him, either seeped into the black of his armor and the clothing beneath or into the bodies below him. Maybe there's still actual ground there too. This use to be a pretty field, tall green-blue grass with the mountains and the trees in the distance. The air up here is ever-cool. It only gets warm for a few hours in the afternoon, when the sun is directly above. Snow is never out-of-season. It had been dawn when we'd arrived, and several of us had crept close to the precipice to watch the sun rise. Danu's side must have mirrored that sentiment, too. We knew they were there, they knew we were, but it wasn't until the sun had cleared the mountains that the House of Dochure's Prince-and-General had made his charge. If my Prince-and-General is in attendance, we never attack first.

I smile at Danu. He would be the type of man to revel in a sun rise.

"Prince, Counsel, I've found him!"

The sound of armor grinding against itself is earsplitting suddenly. I grimace, clamping my eyes tightly closed. Did it always sound like that?

"Good job, Scout. Now return to the guard and keep an eye out. Prince-and-General Petinst and I will join you shortly."

The sun is blocked and I sense bodies towering above Danu and me. I open my eyes and the man leaning over me jumps back. "By the gods, she's

HERO LOST: MYSTERIES OF DEATH AND LIFE

actually still alive!" Prince-and-General Petinst.

Counsel appears behind him. Glances over Petinst's shoulder. "Not for long."

They walk over me, to Danu. I count the seconds between my breaths. Five. I'm fine. They walk over Danu, a boot crushing his hand and snapping the bones in the process.

"What was that?" Petinst cries out.

"Your boot. You broke his hand."

Petinst laughs. He searches for the other one but it's on Danu's stomach. He can't step on it and break it there. He kicks the body instead, winces and gasps at the strength of Danu's armor.

"His head, Prince-and-General Petinst. You came for his head. You have to show your parents, have to send a message to Dochure that their prince is dead. That we have claimed victory. You won the war."

My fierce Prince-and-General draws his sword, nodding and staring fixedly at Danu's neck, rocking quickly foot to foot.

"Take off the helmet," Counsel instructs.

"I'd have to touch him!" Petinst drops the sword tip onto Danu's shoulder. The armor deflects it and Petinst almost loses his balance.

"Yes."

"Why?!"

"So that it doesn't get in the way and make things difficult for you. You can put it on again after."

"Then I'd have to touch him again! Touch his *severed head*!"

Counsel releases a controlled huff of irritation. "We have to hurry. Right to the neck. It'll go straight through."

Petinst lifts the hilt of his sparkling sword to his waist. It's not high enough. Not for someone with no muscle mass or strength. His blade has rarely even kissed the air. What if it's not even sharp? He brings it down and I shut my eyes, cringing. The sword tip lodges into something just at my nose. Something sprays over my face. I open my eyes to Danu's destroyed jaw. He is handsome no more.

Nine seconds.

"It didn't go through! Uh," he gags. Stops himself. Gags again before turning his head sharply to the side and vomiting all down Danu's black-armored body. It had glistened in the sunlight. Before I'd attacked him. I would never have agreed that black armor could ever be striking, but it was beautiful on him and his men.

"I can't do it," Petinst pouts.

"You can. You will. A man's word is never enough. You must have something to prove that you killed him. That he is unquestionably dead. Hurry now before someone sees. Put your back into it. Hit him again."

"I don't want to!"

"Your parents will know if you lie. This is why I can't do this for you this time. You have to."

I turn my head away.

Stare at the sky above. The sun has shifted, over the trees and politely out of my eyes.

The sword comes down. More retching. Swearing. Arguing.

I count my breaths.

The sword comes down two more times.

Eleven seconds. I counted twice. Consistent is good. It's good.

"It'll look like you fought him viciously, I assure you."

"You should have done this, Counsel! You purposely make me look like a fool! I'm going to be sick again."

"You'll be fine. Let's go. Grab his head. And the helmet. I'll take his sword. That thing's worth something."

"I'm not touching his head!"

"Ok, ok. I'll grab his head. You carry his helmet and the swords."

"Swords?"

"Yes. *Yours* and *his*...Prince-and-General Petinst."

"There isn't enough blood on my sword to prove I'd done it! He didn't have any left! My parents will never believe that I killed him!"

His voice is grating. Had I never noticed? Maybe he never actually spoke to us. Maybe it's been Counsel's orders trickling down through the ranks instead. Maybe I just became accustomed to tuning my ineffectual Prince-and-General's voice out. Danu would've taken his head in one mild stroke. One handed.

No, the General-Prince of Dochure would have been embarrassed for him, for my kingdom, and would have packed him up and sent him home to exile in protected shame. He'd have provided an escort, too.

Twelve seconds.

"It's fine. No one will question it. We'll say you cleaned it up on the way home."

Why wouldn't Danu and his parents have had his sisters under as heavy a guard as his wife? That was in the overheard conversation as well. Danu's wife was their main target. They searched for seven months. She would have been publically shamed and then executed to psychologically crush the House of Dochure.

"No. No, I want the sword that killed him. She must be lying on it."

A pause in their voices. When will they leave? My brain is a whirlwind and Petinst and his counsel are exhausting. I close my eyes and retreat within my skin and armor again. I use to love my armor. Now it's annoyingly restrictive, ill-fitting, and burdensome. Much like my Prince. Oh! That's actually funny!

BREATH BETWEEN SECONDS

"Counsel!"

"Yes, Prince-and-General Petinst?"

"I'm not going to touch her! Find me her sword! I saw her fighting him with one. She must be on top of it."

Counsel grunts under his breath and lowers himself to my side. I don't know much about him. Is he honorable? I watch him, numb and unmoving as he rifles around, hitting my legs to the side, lifting my shoulder to check beneath me, rolling me towards him by my hip to check beneath my left side, letting me crash back to a semblance of my previous position. Disjointed and discomfited. The alteration is mind-numbingly uncomfortable, bringing new jolts of pain. I frown. It's *my* sword! It took me months to save up enough to have it designed and made. It has never been handled by anyone other than that blacksmith and myself. I hope it takes their hands.

Counsel grabs mine and wrenches them from my side, and bright red blood shoots up to paint him. I gasp, the swift answering pain and the sense of flow and loss both relieving and terrifying.

He leans away, his eyes wide but blank.

Sixteen seconds.

"Well, she'll be dead even quicker now, Counsel. I don't want her sword anymore. It'll be covered in *her* blood."

Counsel wipes my blood from his hands over his clean silver armor and backs up onto his feet. "Fine. The sun's setting. Let's move before any of their scouts show up. We've got to get you home, too."

"Yea. Yea. I want to go home. Don't forget his head."

"Of course, Prince-and-General Petinst."

A jagged edge of Danu's vertebra scrapes across my nose as Counsel walks over me. I can't breathe, can't complete either an in or an out. Can't count my breaths, can't hold my side in. I stare, unblinking, straight up. My heart is frenetic, jumping around my chest in a panic. At least it's still beating. That's always a good thing.

Petinst's and Counsel's armor screech as their boots crunch over bodies. Their voices, their laughter, amplify just when they should diminish entirely. Counsel will have raised Danu's head in triumph for all my waiting former comrades to cheer under. Petinst will have been sufficiently congratulated so that his lie will have been swept away.

I look at Danu's corpse, but his corpse is gone. He's sitting beside me with his legs crossed and no display of urgency or fear on his face as he counts my breaths.

"Twenty...three...seconds," I inform him. I can count my own breaths. I frown at Danu and he smiles. He really is a handsome man. His wife, wherever she is hiding, must be beautiful as well. To see them together would be blinding. Their people must be devoted to them-not like my people are devoted to our House. We have no choice. His people, I think they choose every day, and they delight in their choice.

Rumors and reputations. The man beside me had none but his devotion to his sisters, and the man I followed has a fabricated one that no one will challenge. How ignorant and blind are my House's rulers that they would award him power and control over their army? I won the war for my House, but my House does not deserve to win.

I begin to laugh. It doesn't hurt this time, but I cough on something thick and metallic-tasting that defies gravity to leak upwards out of my body.

Thirty seconds.

I laugh harder and Danu nods, standing up to leave. This has been a long, tough day. I collapse once more within myself. My armor is now an exoskeleton, holding me together. I'll rejoin my troupe in awhile. After I rest.

The sky is orange and blue, purple, pink. I've never watched the sun set before. I smile, watching the sky go kaleidoscope until my vision blackens out.

I count the breaths between my seconds...

One...

The End

L. Nahay writes mostly in the fantasy genre, with a focus on female characters redetermining what 'being strong' means. Her focus is real-world traumas written within the vastness that is fantasy, preferring both the limitlessness of possibilities, and the clearance to challenge the boundaries of imagination that the genre provides. Her first novel, *Red Moonglow on Snow*, was released in 2013. She is currently working on several different stories--in whatever spare time she can steal while raising two monsters (who swear they're actually human teens).
www.facebook.com/LNahayauthor/
www.instagram.com/l.nahay/

The Insecure Writer's Support Group was founded by science fiction author Alex J. Cavanaugh in September, 2011. Its purpose - to encourage, support, and inform. The website is a database resource for writers and authors, with weekly guests and tips, thousands of links, and a monthly newsletter. There is also a monthly bloghop the first Wednesday of every month and a Facebook group.

Website: www.insecurewriterssupportgroup.com
Facebook: www.facebook.com/groups/IWSG13
Twitter: www.twitter.com/TheIWSG
Email: admin@insecurewriterssupportgroup.com
Newsletter signup: http://insecurewriterssupportgroup.us12.list-manage.com/subscribe?u=b058c62fa7ffb4280355e8854&id=cc6abce571

CPSIA information can be obtained
at www.ICGtesting.com
Printed in the USA
FSOW01n0017230417
33367FS